Heiress Bride

CYNTHIA WOOLF

ISBN:1938887220
ISBN-13: 978-1-938887-22-2

DEDICATION

For Jim, my wonderful husband. I couldn't do this
without you. I love you.

.

CONTENTS

ACKNOWLEDGMENTS

For my critique partners, Michele Callahan, Karen Docter, Kally Jo Surbeck-Owren and Jennifer Zane, thank you ladies. Your thoughts and assistance have been invaluable in writing and finishing this book. You're the best.

Thanks to my editor, Kally Jo Surbeck-Owren. How lucky am I, my editor is also one of my critique partners. Thank you so much for all you do and both hats that you wear for me.

.

CHAPTER 1

March 14, 1871

Dear Mrs. Selby,

It is my understanding from your last correspondence that you have found a bride for me. Enclosed with this letter is a draft in the amount of one hundred dollars to cover both your fee and the train ticket for a certain Miss Ella Davenport. One way from New York City to Denver, in the Colorado Territory.

Thank you for your assistance in this matter. Sincerely,

Nathan Ravenclaw

Margaret Selby placed the letter into Nathan Ravenclaw's file. His file was thicker than most. She sighed. He'd been more difficult to help than she'd originally thought he would be. He was a successful rancher, it was true, but because of his half Arapaho Indian heritage, he was outcast from both the white and the Arapaho communities. Especially when it came to marriage prospects. They might begrudgingly accept him in business, but not to marry their sisters or daughters.

She wasn't certain she was going to be successful until young Ella Davenport came into her office. Ella was a beautiful young woman with chocolate brown eyes and dark brown hair. In a cruel twist of fate she'd been horribly disfigured in a carriage accident and was now a recluse from her society because of those scars.

Margaret thought these two young people could, perhaps, help each other to heal. She felt this one deep in her bones. This was the right match for both of them.

She placed the draft in her reticule and then readied herself for the short walk to the bank. Her black coat was made of fine wool to withstand the harsh winter wind that whistled between the buildings. She pulled the bright blue scarf over her fiery red hair. Her glorious hair that held not a trace of gray in it, despite having reached the age of thirty-five. The scarf was the only splash of color in her entire outfit, even her gloves were black. She blew out the lamp on her desk and closed the door behind her.

Her philandering husband had been kind enough to bequeath her this beautiful building before he died in the bed of his mistress. He hadn't managed to give her children, which he never forgot to tell her was her fault, but he left her with a place to run her business and to live. She supposed she should be grateful for that.

Her apartment was on the second floor of the three story building. The third floor she rented to a young couple for two dollars and fifty cents per month. One quarter of the market rent of ten dollars

3

a month. As part of their rent, the young man did upkeep on the building. It was a beneficial arrangement for all concerned.

She hurried the two blocks to the bank. A storm was fast approaching and she wanted to be safely tucked in her apartment before it enveloped the city.

Miss Davenport was due in the office tomorrow afternoon to pick up her tickets for the trip to Denver. In the morning, if weather permitted, Margaret would go to the train depot and buy the tickets Miss Davenport would need to get her to Denver, in the Colorado Territory.

She entered the bank at close to closing time. It was quiet. The local businesses had not ended their workday and she timed it specifically for that reason. She went to the first open teller, deposited the draft and withdrew the money for the train ticket.

Shoving the money into her reticule, she braced for the cold walk back home.

*****

The storm passed in the night leaving a dusting of snow and clear blue skies. Ella Davenport dressed with care for her final meeting with Mrs. Selby. Her black wool skirt and matching jacket were fitted perfectly. She eschewed the bustle that was popular, preferring instead a simple A-line skirt. She had her blouses made with a high, straight collar to hide her scars. Her blouses were all plain white. Nothing to attract attention to her face. Even here at home, she was conscious of her facial scars. Today she would go out wearing a heavy veil. It was easier to wear the thick lace than to see the look on people's faces when they saw her disfigurement. At first horror, and then pity. She hated it.

Today she would get her train tickets for the trip west to the Colorado Territory and Mr. Nathan Ravenclaw.

She went down to the breakfast room. It was one of her favorite rooms. The soft blue walls above the chair rail with the dark blue flowered wall paper below appealed to her need for calm. She knew that Cook prepared her favorites for her. Eggs, sausage and mushroom toast.

Joshua was already there dressed in one of his suits. This one brown, the same caramel color as his eyes. Her brother was a handsome man in a quiet way.

"Good morning, Brother."

"Good morning. You look particularly fetching this morning."

"It's my final meeting with Mrs. Selby. I get my tickets today."

Joshua put down his paper and stared at her. "Are you certain this is the right course of action for you? There are dozens of men who would be happy to marry you."

"You mean they would be happy to marry my money. Or, worse yet, to marry me out of pity. I don't want a marriage based on either one of those things. Mr. Ravenclaw knows about my scars, but Mrs. Selby said he carries scars of his own because of his heritage. Being half Arapaho Indian has outcast him from both the whites and the Indians.

Though they might not be visible he still has them."

"Have you thought about the fact that if you marry this man, you'll then be outcast as well?"

She finished filling her plate and sat down on her brother's left. It had become her habit to sit there so he wouldn't have to look at her scars while he ate. He'd never asked her to do it. Her scars didn't bother him for the most part, though she occasionally saw pity in his eyes. Then it was gone as quickly as it came.

She sat down, filled her fork with the savory mushroom toast and then set it down again, her appetite suddenly gone. "Have you not looked at me lately?" She circled in front of her face with her hand. "Do you not see the scars on the left side of my face? Do you not see that I have my collars made especially high to cover the ones on my neck? If these are the ones you can see, have you never wondered at the ones you can't? Not only those on my body, but those inside? Am I not already an outcast?"

Resigned to her decision, he nodded. "Well,

if you're sure, I will support you. If it doesn't work out you can always come back here. You will always have a home here with me." He took a deep breath. "I want to have your trunks shipped to you so you don't have to deal with them when you change trains. From the research I've done, the trip takes seven days and you'll have to change trains at least twice."

"I know. I'm prepared. I have one valise with me with a change of clothes in it. I'll put those on just before I reach Denver. I believe that's the last stop. Mr. Ravenclaw will meet me there. I've had cook prepare some bread and cheese to take with me and I have cash to buy food wherever it's possible. I understand that there are women who make money selling box lunches to train passengers in some of the towns we'll be stopping at. I intend to take the tickets Mrs. Selby gives me and upgrade them to a sleeping car. There is no need to be primitive before I have to be." She smiled. "Listen to me rattle on."

Joshua smiled back. He always told her that

her smile transformed her face. That it was so beautiful no one noticed the scars, only her rare beauty.

He set his coffee cup back in the saucer. "I haven't seen you this excited since," he shook his head, "I don't remember the last time."

"I am excited. I'm finally getting on with my life. The accident is not going to be what defines me."

"I only wish they'd caught the man who sabotaged the carriage. You could have died just as father did." She watched the color rise up his neck as he tried to keep his anger in check before he slammed his fist on the table. "I'm sure you were meant to."

"Probably, but I didn't. I'm sure it was MacGregor or one of his henchmen who sawed through the carriage axels. They had to be trying to kill us. He's always wanted the business. Ever since Father bought him out and the business boomed. He wanted back in, but Father said no. You remember that."

"Yes, I remember. I also remember he tried to court you before the accident and kept coming around until you told him to stop. Did you believe that he might be responsible?"

"It occurred to me but that's not why I didn't want his suit. I mean, my God, he's father's age," she said, incredulous that he would even have thought she might be interested. "You're going to have to be extra careful, Joshua." She placed her hand on his arm and squeezed. "He's going to try to kill you, too."

He patted her hand. "Now, we don't know that."

"If we don't know it, why do you have James and Robert? They're your bodyguards. Mine too, if I stayed. I should be safe now that I'm leaving."

"I'll be fine. Eat your breakfast and check your hair again. It's falling on one side."

"What?" She got up from the table and went to one of the many mirrors that lined the north dining room wall. They made the room seem bigger than it was.

"There's nothing wrong with my hair, you ornery cuss."

He laughed. "Now, now. Such language coming from my sweet sister."

She laughed now, too. "There is nothing sweet about your sister and you know it."

"So you say."

He had a twinkle in his eye and a smile on his beloved face. She would miss him more than she could say. Though she'd never told him, she was pretty sure he already knew it. They were as close as a brother and sister could be. The carriage accident that took their father and scarred Ella had only brought them closer together. Just the thought of their father, gone only a year, still hurt. Her heart literally ached when she remembered him and all they used to do together. She still shivered at the thought of her near demise.

Joshua had been at her bedside every day while she was in the hospital recovering from all the surgeries and then he'd stayed with her when she

11

came home. He never winced when he looked at her, though she was sure he wanted to. Everyone did, at least the first time. Friends with empathy at all the pain she must have gone through, strangers at the ugliness of her transformed face.

The veil helped when she traveled outside the house. People were less likely to be horrified by her visage if it was shadowed by the veil. That was another reason for the sleeper cabin, a Pullman car if she could get one, to save other people's sensibilities. Price wasn't an object. She could afford what she wanted, but she wasn't willing to buy a husband. She much preferred the idea that a man was willing to accept her knowing about her scars. Even willing to pay for her hand in marriage. Though some would say she's a bought woman, she didn't think of it like that. It was a contract between two people and a hope for her future. One she didn't have if she stayed in New York.

Ella prepared to journey into the cold and visit Mrs. Selby. She put on her long, black wool coat, pulled her black wool scarf over her head and around the lower half of her face. Traveling in the cold was easier for her than in warm weather because she could cover the lower half of her face with her scarf and no one thought anything about it. She'd pulled on her winter boots. Lined in soft fur, they kept her feet warm even in the snowy streets.

The walk to Matchmaker and Co. was about a mile, but Ella refused to be in a carriage unless absolutely necessary. The accident had given her a fear of enclosed spaces and carriages in general, that she hadn't had before. She wasn't sure how the train ride would be. Yet another reason for the Pullman. She had to get to the station and reserve at the very least a sleeper cabin with some privacy. There was no way she could travel in the main cabin with everyone else, sitting up the whole way for seven days. She had to be able to remove the veil for as long as possible, for simple comfort. It was heavy and the air circulation was not the best.

After about twenty minutes of walking, she reached Mrs. Selby's office and went in. The warmth welcomed her. A coal stove in one corner flooded the room with heat.

Mrs. Selby sat at her desk in the middle of the room. Behind her were tables stacked neatly with hundreds of files.

She looked up. "Come in. Come in, Ella. So glad you could make it. Sorry to get you out on such a terrible day, but I have your tickets and you leave day after tomorrow. I hope you're packed."

"Thank you, Mrs. Selby. I am. I started packing as soon as I knew you'd accepted my application. I have to ask again, are you sure Mr. Ravenclaw is aware of the extent of my scars? I don't want him surprised when he sees me."

"Rest assured, my dear, he has full knowledge and has no qualms about a woman with scars of any kind. In his mother's culture they are a 'mark of bravery' I believe he said."

Ella neared the stove, the cold suddenly seeming greater. "Bravery, no. Survival, yes."

"You are too harsh with yourself, Ella," scoffed Mrs. Selby.

"I don't think so. I survived. My father did

not."

Mrs. Selby nodded. "I understand. I also know that it's been difficult for you. But that's all in the past. There's a new life waiting for you, Ella. Take advantage of the opportunity being offered."

"Oh, I intend to. I still have some arrangements to make, so I will leave now." She walked to the older woman and gave her a hug. "Thank you."

Mrs. Selby hugged her back. "I wish you the very best, Ella. You and Nathan will make a great marriage. Just remember that it takes work. Don't expect everything to be perfect, at least in the beginning."

"I'll remember."

Ella left and found a carriage. "To the train depot please."

It was too far to walk in this bone chilling cold, or she wouldn't have taken it. As soon as she got inside, the clawing fear started. She opened the curtains and the window, letting in the chilly but fresh air. Better to deal with the weather than the dark fear causing sweat to trickle down her back and her stomach to curdle.

Once at the train depot she asked the driver to wait. Inside she went to the ticket window.

"I'd like to exchange these tickets, please."

"We don't normally do that, Miss. They are not refundable."

"I don't want them refunded. I want to upgrade them to a private car, or at least a Pullman sleeper car, for the entire trip."

"Oh, in that case, I'm sure I can help you. Let me see your tickets, please."

Ella handed him the tickets and he made the changes necessary. She paid the difference and he handed new tickets back to her.

"I hope you have a very good trip, Miss."

"Thank you. I'm sure I will."

*****

Ella stayed mostly in her compartment where she could rest without the veil. It was a double edged sword. She was confined to the sleeper compartment or to the veil. Both were stifling, but at least there was a modicum of freedom without the heavy lace restricting her.

She did have to go out to use the bathroom in the main passenger car and to the dining car to eat. She got off the train at every stop she could and got fresh air. At night she would go to the platform between the cars to feel the air rush at her and though her hair without fear of being seen. In the dark, she didn't worry that her scars would bother anyone.

She arrived in Denver on April 6, 1871. A date she would forever remember as the start of her life. It was almost like another birthday.

The weather was cold. The wind rushed off the plains and collided with the mountains to the west, keeping the chill in the air. The buildings weren't as tall as in New York, but the wind still whistled between them and over the platform where she stood. She was glad of her good wool coat and lined boots. They kept her warm while she waited for Mr. Ravenclaw to find her. There wasn't anyone else wearing a veil so she didn't think he'd have much problem identifying her.

She wasn't really sure what she expected, but it wasn't the tall, devastatingly handsome man that approached her. He had a square jaw shaved clean and a tiny dimple in his chin. Black eyebrows slashed over his eyes, the color of which was hidden by the shadow from his hat, pulled low on his head. For once she was glad of her veil. He wouldn't be able to see her mouth hanging open, gawking at him.

"Miss Davenport?"

"Yes. Are you Mr. Ravenclaw?"

"I am."

Ella was surprised to find her hand trembled as she held it out to him. "Ella Davenport."

He removed his glove and enveloped her hand in his big one. His fingers brushed the skin of her wrist just above her glove. The tingle that traveled clear to her toes was unexpected and her gaze snapped up to his. She looked up into the most beautiful blue eyes. They seemed to question the chemistry between them as much as she did.

He held her hand for what seemed like a lifetime and they simply starred at each other.

"Miss Davenport...."

"Ella. Please."

"Ella. I would like for you to lift your veil."

"Are you sure you wish to do this in public. It can be...shocking."

"I'm sure." He squeezed her hand and then let go.

"Very well." She lifted the heavy lace, prepared for him to be taken aback by the ugliness of it. She wasn't prepared for him to lift his hand and gently trace the thin, putrid purple scar all the way from her left eye over her cheek and down her neck to the top of her collar.

There was no disdain on his face. His blue eyes took in everything and accepted it, but even so he said the last thing she expected.

"You are a very beautiful woman."

She stood there with her mouth open until he raised her chin with his knuckle.

"Why are you surprised? Surely you have

heard the compliment before."

She shook her head to clear it and find her tongue. "Not since the accident, except from my brother. But he's biased. He loves me."

"He but states the obvious. Your scars do not detract from your beauty."

"I must thank you because good manners dictate it. However, I believe we should see about getting you some glasses."

He laughed. A rich, deep baritone. "I'm glad you have a sense of humor."

"Who was joking?"

He laughed again. "Where are your trunks?"

"They're being shipped. Joshua, my brother, didn't want me to have to deal with them while changing trains."

"Very smart. They will be delivered to Golden. Freight comes all the way there."

"But not people? How odd."

"Yes, you'd think they could add a passenger car. I'm sure they will soon."

"What are the plans now? Are we to marry here or in Golden City?"

"I thought we could visit the Justice of the Peace while we're here and then get to know each other a bit on the way to the ranch."

He picked up her valise and headed to a wagon parked at one end of the platform. "I brought the buckboard anticipating you having trunks. I would have brought the carriage otherwise. It's more comfortable."

"Please don't apologize. I prefer the open wagon."

He cocked his head to one side in question.

She explained. "My accident was in a carriage. I was trapped inside for quite a while before they could get me out."

"No wonder you don't like riding in a carriage."

They were at the buckboard. A simple wagon with a bench seat in front of a large flat bed with raised sides. The rear panel opened to allow for easier loading of freight or supplies.

"It's not just carriages, but enclosed spaces of any kind. I much prefer the open air around."

"As do I. The first fifteen years of my life were spent with my mother's people. I slept outdoors whenever the weather permitted and sometimes when it didn't." He smiled and her stomach did a little flip.

He helped her up to the bench, lifting her as if she weighed no more than a sack of potatoes. She enjoyed the feel of his big hands on her waist. He made her feel feminine for the first time in a long time.

He went around the back of the wagon and climbed up to the bench.

"Giddyup." He slapped the reins on the hindquarters of two matched blacks. Some of the finest looking horses she'd ever seen.

"Your horses are beautiful."

"Thank you. Caught them myself."

"Caught them?"

"There are wild mustangs that roam the mountains north of here. I went up with some of my ranch hands and we caught about ten of the animals and brought them back. Some were easier to break than others. These two took to the bit right away and then to the harness as well."

"I guess I never really thought about how horses are trained."

"Now you know." He pulled the wagon to a stop due to heavy traffic and then started up again.

She couldn't think of anything to say, so stayed quiet, both of them reflecting on what was about to happen.

About a quarter of an hour later he pulled up in front of a large three story stone building. "Here's the Justice's office."

He came around and helped her down. That tingle was back and it was darn disconcerting. She lowered her veil.

"You can leave it off."

"No." She shook her head and let the heavy veil fall into place. "You don't know how people react. It is not something pleasant to see."

He took her hand. "Very well, but after we

are married, you will wear the veil no more. You will be my wife and I take pride in that."

"You're crazy. People back up when they see me. I don't like that. I won't wear it at home or with people who know us. Perhaps, eventually I won't wear it at all, but I need time to adjust."

Nathan nodded. "I understand. Some people back up when they see me, too."

"Why? You're the most handsome man I've ever seen."

She watched him redden at her praise, obviously not used to it. "Thank you for the compliment. But that's not what whites see. They see an Indian. A breed. That's what those who don't know me call me. A breed. You may get called names, too. Are you prepared for that?"

She thought about it for a moment before answering. "If you're willing to put up with the comments you'll hear about me, then I'll try to put up with the name calling. But I won't have you disparaging yourself in front of me. You have no need to apologize to anyone."

"Nor do you."

She blushed. It was so much easier to fiercely protect him from perceived injustices than see the ones against herself.

"I suppose I don't. The accident wasn't my fault. As a matter of fact, I don't believe it was an accident."

"You believe someone was trying to kill you?"

"Yes. Both my father and me. Now I worry for my brother's safety. But he is forewarned and has loyal staff and friends, plus two bodyguards." She paused to catch her breath. Looking at her soon to be husband, she added, "And I think Í know who arranged it, but I can't prove it. Yet."

"Why would this person want you dead?"

"He was my father's former business partner. He's been trying to buy back his portion of the business since it became successful. When he sold it, the company, a ship building company, was not profitable. Since the war, it's become very profitable and he wants back in. He even tried courting me to get it. "

"But how would eliminating you and your father change things for him?"

"If he gets rid of all of us, he can buy the ship yard from the probate court at ten cents on the dollar. I'd say that's a motive for murder. My brother has two bodyguards who are with him twenty-four hours a day. I simply left the state. Hopefully, that will keep Angus MacGregor from finding me."

They stopped at the double doors that led into the courthouse and to the Justice of the Peace's office.

Nathan looked at her. "Are you ready?"

Her hands shook so she closed them into fists. "I am. Are you sure this is what you want? I'd understand if you want to change your mind."

He shook his head and smiled. "I'm not changing my mind."

"Neither am I. Let's get this done."

He held the door for her and she walked through to a new life on the other side.

The ceremony was short and sweet. Nathan lifted her veil and gave her the most amazing, gentlest kiss she'd ever had. Before her accident she'd had her share of beauxs. Young men who would sneak a kiss in the shadows of the garden. None of whom continued to come around after the accident. After they'd seen the damage done.

Nathan was different. He didn't cringe. His eyes actually seemed to be filled with passion when he looked at her. Like he was staking a claim. And she guessed he did have a claim to her now. He was her husband. *Husband.* She'd thought she'd never have one. Now this beautiful man was hers and his kiss held the promise of good things to come.

CHAPTER 2

Ella wore her veil until they were out of
Denver, then put it back on when they went through
Golden City. Several men hollered at Nathan as
they passed.

"Hey there, Nathan. Who's that beside you?
That the new missus?" asked a red haired young
man, who ran up beside the wagon as it slowly
passed.

"Yes, Jamie. This is Ella. My wife."

Ella waved at the man as he trotted to keep
up with the wagon. "Nice to meet you, sir."

Jamie laughed loudly. "I ain't no *sir,*
ma'am. I'm just Jamie."

Nathan held the reins of the walking horses in one hand and put his other arm around Ella, resting it on her shoulders. The move was purely proprietary. Showing his claim on her and she didn't mind at all. As a matter of fact, it felt nice to be wanted. "Tell your boss we'll be seeing him on Saturday, as usual."

"Will do," Jamie replied as he stopped and turned toward the feed store. He tipped his hat to Ella. "Nice to meet you, Mrs. Ravenclaw."

She waved at him. They were far enough away that she'd have had to yell for him to hear her and she didn't want to draw any additional attention to herself.

"I bet you're blushing under that veil," said Nathan.

"Why would I be blushing?" she asked, all too aware of his arm still around her waist.

"Jamie and his, shall we say exuberance at meeting you. Everyone knew I was meeting my bride today. He just wanted to be the first to see you."

She laughed. "Yes, well, he was awfully excited, wasn't he?"

Nathan moved his arm and took the reins in both hands again as they left the city behind. She felt a little bereft. She liked his arm around her. Liked that he wanted everyone to know she was his.

As soon as they'd left Golden City behind, Ella took off her hat and veil once again. She shoved the offending apparel under the seat and turned her face to the sun. Its warmth something she'd not felt for a long time.

"Ahh," she said. "That feels so wonderful."

Nathan looked at her and smiled.

"What?" she asked.

"You seem so happy with just a little sunshine on your face. At this rate I'm going to have no trouble pleasing you."

She laughed. "I am easily amused. After nearly a year without feeling the sunshine on my face for more than a moment, this is amazing."

He pulled onto a driveway off the main road. Far up the road, in a little gully up against the foothills sat the ranch buildings. She could make out the two large buildings, one of which she assumed was the house and several smaller buildings.

As they got close, she saw that the ranch house was one story and sprawling. Shaped like a "U" with a courtyard in the center. Nathan pulled up in front of the open center courtyard. They walked through the courtyard straight to the door in the center of the middle side and entered into a foyer there.

"To the right are the parlor, dining room, kitchen and Martha's bedroom," said Nathan. "And to the left are the family bedrooms."

"Let me introduce you to Martha. She's the one who keeps the place running smoothly. I'm sure you'll want to take over some of her duties, but I leave that up to the two of you."

They headed to the kitchen where Ella saw a short, middle-aged woman with beautiful black hair and sparkling brown eyes.

"Ah, you are the missus for my Nathan."

"Your Nathan?" Ella looked back and forth between Nathan and Martha. "Are you his mother?"

Nathan chuckled. "She might as well be. She'd been with me since my father took me from my mother, Singing Bird. You might say Martha is my white mother."

"Now you've got me thoroughly confused. Maybe later you can explain it all to me."

"We'll have plenty of time for that."

Ella turned to Martha. "Please don't let me interrupt your routine. I want to learn all I can. We had a cook, housekeeper and maids in New York, so I'm woefully ignorant, but I want to learn to do things myself. I know I'll need your help so don't worry about me taking over all your duties. That won't ever happen, but I want to learn. Will you teach me?"

"Sure. I'll teach ya. Looks like ya got a keeper, Nathan."

"Thank you, Martha. I think so, too." He placed his hand on Ella's waist. "Let's go drop off your valise and then I'll show you the rest of the property."

They went to the last of the four bedrooms in the other wing of the house. The master bedroom was the largest by far. Next to it was the room Ella would use as a nursery. It was the smallest of the bedrooms. There were two other bedrooms in addition to these two. Plenty of room for children. Babies. The thought make her smile.

Nathan carried her belongings into the room and set them down by the double bed. It was covered with a beautiful patchwork quilt.

"This is gorgeous. Who made it for you?" asked Ella, as she ran her fingers over the quilt and admired the fine detail of the stitches.

"My aunt Sara made it. She's actually my great aunt on my father's side, of course."

"It's lovely and I can tell it took a lot of work to make."

"Yes. I can see bits of shirts that I wore in several different years, so I know she worked on it a long time."

"And the fur rug in front of the fireplace? Did you shoot the animal?"

"It's a buffalo and yes, I killed it, with bow, arrow and spear. It was the first buffalo I got as a man. My mother prepared it for me."

"What do you mean as a man? You were only fifteen when you left your mother's people. That is hardly a man."

"Not in white culture, but as an Arapaho, I'd been a man for a couple of years."

"I see." She didn't, but that would be something for later as well. There were a lot of things for later. Her gaze came back to the bed. "Um, Nathan. We need to discuss something."

He followed her eyes to the bed. "What would that be?"

"I, uh, I think we should get to know each other before we, us, you know."

Nathan knew exactly what she was talking about. It had been on his mind since he'd kissed her that morning. That kiss had been the sweetest in recent memory. His new wife was many things, including, if he wasn't mistaken, a virgin. He hadn't expected that. He didn't know why, but he'd thought that anyone who'd sign up to be a mail order bride would be experienced. But there was no hiding the blush that rose from her collar clear to the top of her head.

"What would that be?"

"You know. I don't think we should be," she stopped and whispered, "intimate yet. Not until we get to know each other better."

Grasping his chin by the thumb and forefinger as though he was contemplating it, he said, "No. I don't think we should put it off."

"But if we decide that we don't suit, we can get an annulment much easier than a divorce."

He dropped his hand and closed the distance between them. "Get one thing straight." He took her by the shoulders. "There will be no annulment and no divorce." Then he brought his mouth down on hers the way he'd wanted to all day. He was gratified when her arms wrapped around his neck and she kissed him back. His tongue pressed against the seam of her lips as he begged for entry.

She eased her lips apart and he entered, slowly, gentling the kiss. Tentatively, she touched her tongue to his and he thought he'd die if he didn't get more. He dueled with her, feasted on her, forgetting she was untried until she pulled back.

"Nathan?" she asked, her breathing hard.

"Ella. I want you, but I'll compromise with you. We sleep together, learn each other's body. I won't take you until you ask me, but I will touch you. Everywhere."

With those words he left her.

*****

Ella sat down on the side of the bed and touched her fingers to her swollen lips. He was going to touch her, had touched her, kissed her and wasn't the least repulsed. But what would he think when he saw the rest of her scars on her neck and shoulder? She had the feeling he wouldn't care. There was no pity in his kiss or in the fire that had been in his eyes.

"Oh, my."

He made her want more out of this marriage than just being comfortable. She wanted it all. She wanted love. But even he, kind as he was, couldn't love her. Could he?

Closing her eyes, she wished it could be. She was very afraid it would be all too easy to fall in love with her husband. He was kind, gentle, fierce and entirely too handsome for her own good.

She took a deep breath and got up, grabbed one of her bags and opened it. There was a door at one end of the room she hoped was a closet. She shook out the skirts and blouses in the bag. Taking a skirt in hand she opened the door. It was a closet and there was even room for her clothes. Well, these clothes. They'd have to figure out something else when her trunks arrived.

She hung her clothes up and looked in the bureau for an empty drawer. Nathan had anticipated it and the top two were empty for her. She put her chemises and bloomers in one drawer, her stockings and second corset in the other. She would be so very happy to get out of her corset.

She hadn't been able to do it by herself. Nathan would have to help her, but the way he looked at her she didn't think he would mind. It didn't take as long to unpack as she thought it would. Her clothes needed ironing after more than a week in the bag. She went down to see Martha.

Wonderful smells wafted out of the kitchen. She followed her nose to the stove. There on top was a pot full of beans and another one full of stew. Her mouth watered and her stomach growled. She'd forgotten until that moment that she'd had nothing to eat today.

"May I have some?" she asked Martha.

"Of course, honey. Here, let me get you a bowl." Martha opened a cupboard to the left of the sink in the corner. Ella saw plates and bowls in the cabinet.

"Do you mind if I look in the cabinets? I need to know where everything is."

"No. Go on ahead and look all ya want. This is yer house now, too. The dishes are in the upper cabinets and pots and pans in the lower one.

We have fifteen men we feed in here along with you, me and Nathan. It gets to be quite boisterous."

"You must use the dining room. The table here isn't large enough."

"Yeah. Nathan says everyone is family and family eats in the dining room. I'll have you help me with dinner. It will help you get familiar better than just looking in cabinets." She bustled about grabbing a bowl from one of the cabinets and a spoon from a drawer under the counter. She quickly filled it with the savory stew from the large pot on the stove.

"I knew I was going to like you, Martha. And you never flinched when you saw my scars. Why? Everyone except Nathan, has at least flinched when they see the scars on my face. Why didn't you?"

Martha handed her a bowl. "There's all kinds of scars, honey. Inside and out. I've seen Nathan's scars. Yours are not different to me. Just part of the life you've had."

"Scars? From what? What kind of scars?"

"Those are questions best answered in the privacy of your bedroom. You can ask him yerself."

Ella closed her eyes and knew she blushed. "Of course. How rude of me."

"Not at all. Ya need to ask questions to learn." She pulled a chair out from under the small work table. "Now sit down and eat. I ken hear yer stomach growl from here. I'll have ta get after Nathan fer that."

"Get after Nathan for what?" he said from the doorway.

"For not feedin' yer bride. She's starving. Listen to her stomach."

Now it was Nathan's turn to blush. He bowed his head and ran his hand around his neck before he looked up at Ella. "I'm sorry. I didn't even think about it. Are you alright? Is Martha feeding you enough?"

"I'm fine. But you need to eat as well, you haven't eaten either."

"You're right." He got a bowl and heaped it

with the steaming stew. Then he pulled biscuits from the bread box. "Would you like some?" He held up a biscuit.

"Oh, yes, please." She turned to Martha. "The stew is delicious. Thank you."

Martha blushed under the praise, but brushed it off. "It's easy ta make, I'll show ya tomorrow. Today you should rest from your trip."

"Actually, after we finish eating, I need an iron and ironing board, if you have one."

"They're in the pantry. But if ya bring me what ya want pressed, I'll do it. Our iron doesn't heat properly and it would be best if I do it for ya."

"But I need to learn. I'll be back down after we finish and you can show me how it's done."

"I'm finished," said Nathan as he rose from the table and took his dishes to the sink. "I've got chores to finish before supper." He bent and gave Ella a kiss on the cheek and walked out of the kitchen whistling.

Ella touched her cheek where he kissed it, expecting to find it burning to the touch. Instead, it was cool and she only burned on the inside.

"Okie dokie. If that's what ya want," said Martha.

"What?" said Ella, giving her head a shake to clear it and remember what she and Martha had been talking about. "Oh, yes, It is. The sooner I start learning how to do things for myself, the better. I don't want you to have to take care of me in addition to everyone else here."

"That's kind of ya, but unnecessary. It's my job to take care of everyone including you. And I like my job. Besides, have ya ever ironed anything before?"

Ella shook her head. "No. But I watched our maids do it once."

"You can watch me. After that, if ya still want to try it, I'll let ya try it on a dish towel before ya do yer clothing."

"Why on a dish towel? Do you iron those?"

"Nope. But if you burn it, it won't matter none."

"Fair enough. I'll go get my clothes."

When Ella got back, Martha had the ironing board set up and the iron on the stove to heat.

"How long do you let it heat?"

"The first time, when it's cold out of the cupboard, I leave it on the stove for five minutes. After that no longer than two minutes and that will depend on what I'm ironing." She touched her finger to the iron. "Okay, it's good and hot. Give me your skirt first."

Ella handed over the bombazine skirt. It was terribly wrinkled and probably needed the most work of any of her clothes. Martha made short work of it. Sprinkling it with water from a mason jar with tiny holes poked in the top, then running the hot iron over it, she never let the iron rest in one place for more than a second.

After she practiced on a dishtowel to Martha's satisfaction, Ella tried it with the blouse and it worked. She also had a skirt, blouse, chemise and bloomers that needed washing. "Martha, do you know how to do laundry or do you send it out?"

Martha choked on a laugh. "Send it out?

You are from the city. Honey, we don't send nothin' out for…nothin'. If we can't do it here, it don't get done. Tomorrow is laundry day. You kin help me and see how it works. The day after that is ironin' day. I'll let you do that since ya know how now. Then there's the cooking that has to be done three times a day, everyday. Not much time for anything, but work. Now that you're here, maybe I can get a day off."

Ella was aghast. "You don't get a day off? Surely you jest."

"Why would I 'jest' about that? There's work to be done and if I don't do it, it don't get done. Nathan and the men have their own work to do. I can't expect them to take over my chores because I want a day off."

"Yes, of course," Ella felt totally ashamed of herself. They'd always had Sundays off for all the servants. She wasn't used to them not having some time for themselves. Of course, they always had plenty of servants to cover for one another if they were sick or needed personal time. One of the other maids could always take over. Ella had learned to cook for Sunday meals, as Cook had the day off to visit her sister.

"I can cook a little," said Ella. "I've never cooked for such a large number of people, but I can increase the recipes. I make a very good Yorkshire pudding to go with my roast beef, if you'd like to try that one night."

"I'm more than happy to have ya cook whatever ya please. What is it anyway? Some sort of sweet dessert?"

"No, it's a baked side dish made with beef drippings and served with roast beef. It's very good."

Martha finished with the potatoes she was peeling. "You can fix it tonight if ya want. We be havin' a roast beef fer dinner. I got potatoes, green beans and carrots I canned last year and peach cobbler fer dessert."

"Sounds wonderful. I'll check the larder. I only need eggs, milk, flour, salt and beef drippings."

Martha wiped her hands on her apron. "Well, we got all that so I guess yer cooking some of supper tonight."

"Thank you, Martha."

"Fer what? Lettin' ya help me with my work? That's my pleasure. Now, you go rest until I call for ya to help. Your trip was long and your night will be even longer."

Ella cocked her head in question, but took her freshly pressed clothes to the bedroom and hung them in the closet. Then she looked at the other bedrooms. One of them would have to be turned into a closet for the clothes that were coming and a sewing room. She may not do much of anything else as far as housekeeping, but she could sew. Her nanny had loved to sew. She passed that love on to Ella. She made all of her own clothes.

It wasn't fashionable for a society woman to sew, but it had saved Ella's sanity after the accident. When she couldn't go out in society without a veil, she spent a lot of time at home. There was only so much reading she could do without going crazy, so she sewed. By the time she'd left for Golden, she had an entirely new wardrobe. She hadn't ever worn most of the clothes that were in the trunks that were coming.

Excited about something now, she checked the closet with Nathan's shirts. She could make him a new shirt. Maybe one in blue to go with his eyes. That would be on her list when they went to town.

She went into the bedroom and lay down on the bed suddenly very tired. It was as though all the excitement of the day came crashing down on her at once.

When she woke the sun was low in the sky, dusk setting in. Nathan came into the bedroom, hat in hand. He tossed it on the hat tree next to the door.

"I wondered where you were. I'm glad you were able to rest. Martha said you're making some of supper tonight so I thought I should check on you," he said.

"Yes, supper." She put her feet over the

side of the bed and stretched as she got up. "I didn't think I needed to rest, but it does seem to have revived me. Now to supper, at home we would have called it dinner."

"Here dinner is at noon or one o'clock and supper is in the evening. You'll get used to the different names for things. I did."

"You? But weren't you raised here?"

"No, my father was from Philadelphia. A lawyer out here for a hunt. To make a long story short, he met and fell in love with my mother, but my grandfather, my mother's father, refused to let them marry. Father went back to Philadelphia not knowing Mother was pregnant with me. When he returned a year later and found out, he again wanted to marry her, but she had already married my stepfather."

"So, why did your father wait so long to take you with him?"

He shrugged his shoulders. "It was an agreement they made. Father was adamant that I learn both worlds. It was agreed that when I was fifteen I would go with him. He came every year, so it wasn't like he was a stranger to me. It was difficult, but he overcame all the obstacles, not the least of which was my grandfather, in order to be with me. In the end, because I was a man, it was my choice to go with my father. I could have refused, despite the agreement that was made."

"He sounds like a good man."

"He is. That's why I went with him. Why I chose to know the people he is a part of."

"Your father is still living?"

"Yes. Still in Philadelphia and he still comes out every year. He'll be coming back in a couple of months."

"Does he know you married?"

"Not yet. Figured I'd surprise him."

"Oh, I'm sure he'll be surprised when he sees me. He'll wonder if you were blind when you said 'I do'."

Nathan took a deep breath. "I wish you would not disparage yourself so. I've told you, you are a beautiful woman."

"And I know better." She circled the air in front of her face with her hand. "I see this face in the mirror every day. I remember the reactions of the people who saw me the first time I went out after my bandages were removed. There was horror on their faces and in their eyes. That's how most people see me, Nathan. I don't understand why you don't."

He stood to the side of the door never really coming into the room. Now he leaned onto the door jamb. "And everyone sees me as a breed, a savage. My mother's people are not savages. I'm as much a savage as you are."

She smiled hesitantly, her hands locked in the shirt she held. "I can see that. I have to admit I read some dime novels on the way here and they may have clouded my judgment, some."

He shook his head in disgust. But there was something else in his eyes. Was it fear? Did he think she'd believe those novels? Did she?

"I can only imagine what's in those things. Exaggerations at best and outright lies at worst. I would bet more of the latter."

Ella fingered the shirt she'd brought out of the closet. "I'm sure you're right. I wanted to ask you if I can borrow one of your shirts."

"Why?"

"I want to make you a shirt and I need it for measurements. I can make a pattern from it."

"You sew?" Then he got a twinkle in his eye and said, "I thought all spoiled rich girls did was drink tea with their pinkie in the air."

"Oh, I do that too." She held her pinkie in the air like she had a cup of tea and laughed. "But I like to sew. I'd also like to take the bedroom closest to the foyer and turn it into a sewing room and a place to put some of the things that will arrive with my trunks."

He leaned against the door jam, his arms crossed in front of him. "How many trunks are you expecting?"

"Six. Assuming Joshua didn't add anything."

"Six! How many clothes do you have?"

She shook her head. "Oh no, it's not just clothes, though there are plenty of those. It's quilts and bed linens and my mother's china, my entire hope chest. That's another reason I want that room. So I'll have some place to put it all until I get it put away in the house."

She couldn't help but admire him, looking relaxed with his shirt sleeves rolled up revealing strong tanned forearms. Arms that could hold her and wrap her in the warmth even the affection she so craved.

"So serious. What are you thinking, Ella?" He pushed away from the door and came to her. He took his knuckle and raised her chin until she looked at him. "I won't hurt you." Then he kissed her. He didn't touch her with anything but his lips and that one hand which had managed to somehow work its way behind her head and hold her while he kissed her. She stood there, frozen in place by the feel of his lips on hers. Why was it she forgot everything when he kissed her?

He broke off and rested his forehead against

hers. "You sorely tempt me, Ella." He turned and walked out of the room leaving her still feeling his kiss all the way to her toes.

*****

He'd missed her again. Taking out Father was a good thing and, if it had worked, it would have killed her too, but it didn't. She survived the accident. He'd been unable to get to her after that. Too many people around her all the time.

Regardless, he would find her. Then she would die and he'd be that much closer to owning Davenport Shipping. He could prove his lineage; Father had given him the documents on his last birthday, just before the accident, finally acknowledging him. It had been his mother's last wish and Father couldn't deny her. Father had felt guilty, after all these years and the woman he loved was dying so he relented. But Daniel didn't want to share. He wanted it all. He deserved it all.

Now, however, his new target was preparing to go to the office. He had those two bodyguards with him all the time. No matter. Bodyguards

53

could be bought. He just needed the right persuasion. He would find the Achilles heel for each one of the guards. After they were out of the way, taking care of his little brother, Joshua, would be easy, then all that would stand in his way was Ella. Dear, sweet, ugly Ella. Before he killed Joshua, he needed to find out where Ella went. He knew she'd left. He'd gotten that much from the maid he was sleeping with. The things he did. He shook his head. It didn't matter. She was a pretty little thing. A nice whore, just like all women. Made for only one thing...a man's pleasure.

He laughed thinking about Ella. She'd gone from beautiful swan to ugly duckling in a few lucky strokes of wood from the carriage. But not lucky enough. It hadn't killed her. That damn carriage fell apart and she hadn't died. No, instead they'd found her in the rubble and stitched her back together. It had taken her months to heal. Months when she didn't leave the house. Then, miraculously, she started leaving, walking, always walking, and wearing a heavy veil, one you couldn't see through. Hiding her once beautiful face.

Then, finally, his luck seemed to have turned. He saw trunks being loaded into a delivery wagon. He followed it to the train station.

He went up to the freight master. "Where are these trunks headed?"

"Golden City."

"Where is that?"

"Colorado Territory. A way out west."

"How long will it take them to get there?"

"If there are no delays, it'll take 'em seven days. But we only guarantee 'em in ten."

He thanked the man and handed him two dollars for his trouble and his silence. Joshua would wait. Time to buy a ticket to Golden City, Colorado Territory. Seven days on the train was not something he looked forward to.

Shaking his head he thought, "The things I do for...my rightful place in society."

*****

Supper was a success. Everyone liked her Yorkshire pudding. Even she was pleased with the way it turned out. It was getting late. She and Nathan retired to the parlor after supper. She told him about her life before the accident.

"I was the belle of the ball. My dance card was always full and I had lots of girlfriends, too. Until the accident. Oh, they came to see me in the hospital and even at home while the bandages were safely on. Once the scars were visible, they stopped coming. Fear kept them away. Fear they would have to be seen with me if they kept coming around." She was bitter and couldn't keep it out of her voice, though she tried.

They sat before the fire in two leather covered wing chairs. Nathan held his hand out to her and she put hers in his. "They couldn't have been very good friends if they let something like scars scare them away."

"Oh, I agree with you. I thought they were good friends, but I was proved wrong. They were only my friends while I was popular."

He squeezed her hand. "I won't let you go because of your scars. They don't scare me or repulse me. Do you understand? Your scars are a part of you, no different to me than your brandy eyes."

She'd tried to get the chair on the left so he wouldn't see her scars while they were sitting. Somehow, he'd known what she was about and sat in the chair first. Her scars faced him the whole time they talked and now when he was being so sweet. But she didn't dare trust his word. She'd been burned by too many people. People she thought cared for her. Friends. Beaus.

"It's late and we should go to bed. Morning comes early," said Nathan.

"I suppose we should." She got up and headed back to the bedroom. Once she got there, she stopped in the middle of the room as though she'd forgotten what to do.

With her back to him she asked, "Would you help me out of my corset? I don't have a maid here and I've been wearing it for more than a week now."

"Of course."

She took off her blouse and kept her back to him.

Warm fingers touched the skin above her corset. Then she felt the laces being undone. Once it was done, he opened it and gasped.

"My God, Ella! How have you been able to wear this? It's horrible. You have sores where it's rubbed you raw."

"It's been a little uncomfortable, but I didn't realize there were sores. I'll have to keep it off until they heal."

"Until they heal, my ass. You're never to wear that torture contraption again. You don't need it anyway."

He turned her to face him and she realized he was looking at her and the only thing between her and him was her arms covering her breasts.

"Lower your arms. I want to see what other damage has been done."

"No."

"Ella. I won't attack you. Let me see."

She lowered them.

"Oh, Ella. Such beauty marred by unnecessary damage. Sit on the bed and get off the rest of your clothes. You can put your nightgown on after I've treated your sores. I'll be right back." He left her standing there half naked in the middle of the room. She needed a bath. Badly. It'd been seven full days since her last one and she hadn't been able to change clothes in all that time. The little she'd been able to wash up in the train lavatory wasn't nearly enough.

Ella went to the cheval mirror that stood in the corner of the room by the closet. She looked at her body. Where her corset had ridden up and down under her arms and on the undersides of her breasts were sores, several of them under each arm. Her back had sores all up and down it where the laces pressed into the skin.

She took off her skirt and bloomers. Then she put on her robe but not her nightgown. Nathan wouldn't be able to get to the sores to clean them with her nightgown on. And they needed cleaning. Now that they were exposed to the air, they hurt.

Maybe she'd been too nervous to notice the pain before, but she sure felt it now.

Nathan returned with hot water in a basin and some soft towels. "Here now. Take your robe off and lift your arms."

She did as he asked. Embarrassment kept her looking away from him.

"I can't believe that you didn't feel this. It had to have hurt."

"I think I was too nervous. I certainly feel it now."

He gently washed the affected areas with the hot water, soap and a soft cloth. It stung and burned, but she knew it needed to be done.

"Alright. That's better. I'm going to go get some salve and then you can put on your nightgown."

She looked down at her lap. "Thank you for taking care of me."

He gently took her chin between his thumb and forefinger and raised it so she looked at him. "Ella. You're my wife. I will always take care of you."

She nodded, but kept her eyes lowered.

"Look at me."

Raising her lids she met his intense gaze.

"Trust me, Ella. You're mine now." he said before lowering his lips to hers. He pulled back, "I'm just angry that you were put through such pain. Promise me you won't ever wear that thing again."

"But…"

"No buts. You can't work in it, you can't ride in it, the only thing it's good for is kindling in the fireplace and I don't know if the damn thing would burn."

She laughed. "Probably not."

"Good." He smiled that devastating smile of his and there was a twinkle in his eye. "It's nice to hear you laugh. Let me get that salve."

He left and she realized she'd been sitting there fully naked to the waist. She shook her head in wonder. How could she have not noticed that?

When he returned, she'd pulled her robe up to cover her breasts.

He grinned at her. "Decided to cover those lovelies up, huh? Well, you'll just have to uncover them again; I have to put salve on the poor beauties."

Now she was embarrassed. Thoroughly.

"I'm your husband. I'm allowed to see and touch your body Now, raise your arms again."

She did and he put salve on the sores under her arms, along her back and under her breasts. Wearing the corset for seven days straight without a break had savaged her body. Truth be told, she didn't want to put the thing back on. Nathan forbidding it, though, did make her want to defy him just for spite. She was being ridiculous. The sores needed to heal and wearing the corset wouldn't allow that.

When he finished, he gently raised her robe and covered her up. "You don't know how much it pains me to cover these beauties. You do know you have beautiful breasts don't you?"

She shook her head. "I'd never thought about it. I don't know what other women's look like so I don't have anything to reference them to."

"Trust me. They're gorgeous."

"You say that a lot."

"What?"

"Trust me."

He picked up the dirty towels and the basin.

Then he just grinned at her and left the room.

CHAPTER 3

It was her first night as a married woman. She believed Nathan when he said he wouldn't take her until she asked him to. But she also knew there was only one way to have children and she wanted children more than anything else.

She was sitting on the bed when Nathan came back.

He unbuttoned his shirt and took it off, dropping it to the floor. Ella was greeted by a broad expanse of male chest. Beautiful, caramel colored male chest. He was not unmarred. Above each of his nipples were straight horizontal scars about two inches long. He stopped in front of her.

She reached up and traced them with her fingers.

"Who did this to you?" She was indignant that someone would have wounded him. She was unprepared for the answer.

"I did."

Her gaze snapped up and locked with his. "But why?"

"It is part of a ceremony."

"A ceremony where you harm yourself? That's barbaric." The words were out of her mouth before she could stop them. She slapped her hands over the offending orifice.

His eyes shuttered.

"Nathan. I'm sorry. I didn't mean that. I...."

He held up his hand. "No, don't apologize. We need to get this out. The ceremony I went through is a religious ceremony. The most sacred of all ceremonies to the Arapaho. It is a right of passage. All young Arapaho men go through the Sun Dance ceremony upon entering manhood. It is hoped that you will get a vision during the hanging."

"Hanging?"

"Yes. The skin is pierced with bone. Then a rope is attached to them and the warrior is lifted until he is hanging by the bone. To liberate himself he must tear the skewers through the skin."

She covered her mouth again, this time to control her gag reflex and to stop her from saying something she shouldn't. That didn't stop a quiet whimper from escaping.

He sat next to her on the bed. "Don't be concerned. I got my vision."

"What did you see?"

"You. I saw you."

She was taken aback. "Me? But we just met."

He nodded. "I know. I didn't actually see you, but I saw that I married a beautiful white woman. I didn't believe it was possible so I discarded the message."

"What else did you see in your vision?"

"I saw children and…," he got very quiet. "I saw someone trying to kill you."

"I take it by your silence, they were successful."

"It was just a vision. Nothing more. Part of it came true. I will keep you safe, Ella. But who could want you dead?"

"Just MacGregor. I told you about him."

"This was someone closer to you. Perhaps a family member."

"There is only me and Joshua now. And Joshua is worried about MacGregor as much as I am. He's hired two bodyguards. They're with him day and night."

He put his arm around her shoulder. "You must be tired. It's been a long day for both of us."

She was tired. Her eyelids felt like an anchor was weighing them down. "It has been."

"Then let's go to bed."

"I uh…,"

"Don't worry, you're much too sore for anything other than sleep. But you will sleep in my

67

arms."

Her eyes popped open. "What?"

He smiled. "I may not get to feast on your body tonight, but I can at least hold you."

She swallowed hard as he shed the rest of his clothes and she couldn't help but stare. He was male perfection. His skin was smooth and taunt over hard muscles. She'd already seen his wide shoulders and flat stomach but he also had strong muscular legs and though he might not want to take her, part of his body looked like it was ready to.

He looked down. "Don't worry. I'm in control. You have no need to fear."

She shook her head. "You're beautiful."

"Thank you, but men are supposed to be handsome not beautiful."

"You are that too, but there is no other way to describe your body." Just looking at him made her warm all over.

"I'm glad you think so. A man's wife should always find him attractive. Just as he finds her."

Now she did lower her eyes to her lap.

"Why should that embarrass you?

"Until you, no one has found me attractive in a long time."

"Because they were blind and did not see the treasure in front of them." He came to her on the bed and took her into his arms, "and thank the Gods they didn't or you wouldn't have come to me."

With those words his lips met hers in a scorching kiss. Her tongue automatically came out to duel with his. When they came apart both were breathless.

"When you're healed, we're going to have a wonderful time. If your kiss is any indication, you have untapped passion in you my lovely little wife."

She didn't have any idea what he was talking about, but his words left her pleased and full of desire.

"I'll teach you, Ella. We'll explore and come to know each other's bodies as well as we know our own. But now I want you to rest. Tomorrow will come too soon and it'll be as busy as this one."

*****

She'd left Nathan asleep in their bed. As quietly as she could, Ella pulled the long tin tub off the porch and into the center of the kitchen. She already had two metal buckets full of water heating on the stove. When the water was hot she poured one into the tub and set one to the side. She filled the empty bucket again from the pump at the sink and added the cold water to the tub. Thank God for small favors, at least she didn't have to lug it in from the pump out in the yard.

She added a little more hot water from the bucket beside the tub until the temperature was perfect. She placed a towel and a clean night gown on a chair she brought over from the table and then she undressed leaving her old nightgown in a pile on the floor.

Climbing into the hot water she couldn't stop the small moan of pleasure. She reached up and removed the pins from her hair letting the thick mass fall to the floor. She leaned back and let the hot water relax her. After a few minutes she scooted forward bringing her hair into the water. Then she lay back until her hair was completely submerged and stayed that way, relaxing the tight muscles in her back that were still stiff from the ride in the buckboard from the train station and all the work today that she wasn't used to. Sitting back up she took her precious rose soap she brought with her from New York and scrubbed her hair. She closed her eyes laid back again submerging her hair and rinsing most of the soap from it.

When she opened her eyes she was looking into cool water blue ones attached to the incredibly handsome face of her husband.

She screamed.

He grinned.

Ella sat up quickly covering herself with her arms. "Nathan! What are you doing here?"

"Wondering where you were. I woke and you were gone from our bed."

"Well, you found me. Now go away." She pulled her hair forward over her shoulders hiding the scars on her neck and chest and covering her breast. The thick mass of curls covered her like a dark sable blanket, freeing her hand which dived to her lap.

He shook his head and knelt next to the tub. "I don't think so. You need someone to scrub your back and clean those sores. Give me your soap."

"No." she hissed. "Go away."

He smiled. "I was hoping you'd say that." He plunged his hand into the water finding her legs and pulling his hand up her leg, caressing her as he went.

"Nathan!" she squeaked. "Stop that." She swatted at his hands and he took advantage to replace her hands with his, caressing her mound and eliciting a moan from her. His naked chest rubbed against her back and between his hand and his chest she was lost.

He chuckled and pulled his hand away. "Seriously. Give me your soap and I'll wash your back."

"Just my back and then you'll go away?"

she said handing him her soap.

"Maybe…after I help you rinse your hair."
He lathered his hands and rubbed them up and
down her back. The strokes slow, his fingers gently
kneading the sore, tired muscles with each pass.
Then he brought them around to her front,
massaging her stomach and caressing her as he
moved up to her breasts. Around and around each
one, tweaking her nipples.

She moaned and leaned back into his chest,
giving him access to her. Forgetting for the
moment her scars, her sores, her embarrassment,
she simply felt and enjoyed the pleasure.

He was gentle and thorough. Then he pulled
up her hair and she came back to her senses.

She grabbed her hair. "No. Don't."

"Ella, I've told you, your scars don't bother
me."

"Maybe not, but they bother me." Her head
dropped to her chest. "Please. Don't."

He pulled his hands away from her. "As
you wish. Stand and I'll rinse you."

"I can do it myself."

"Stop being a ninny. I'm trying to help. As soon as you're rinsed, I'll leave you alone."

She looked at him. He was upset with her and yet he still wanted to help her. He was her husband, but she couldn't help her response. She hated her scars. As much as he said they didn't matter, they did to her, but she stood anyway. He poured the contents of the bucket by the tub over her head and rinsed the soap from her hair and body. Then he handed her the towel, turned on his heel and left her alone.

She dried herself quickly put on her fresh nightgown, cleaned up the kitchen and then went to their bedroom. Nathan was still up, lying in bed with the covers riding low on his waist and his hard, naked chest staring at her, reminding her again how beautiful he was.

"Come to bed, Ella, but leave your nightgown off."

"Why?"

"I want to see how the sores from that

torture contraption you wore are healing. Don't worry, I'm not going to make love to you, but I am going to hold you. I want you to get used to my body, to our bodies together. I want to learn every inch of you and for you to learn me. Scars and all. Let me ask you, do my scars bother you? Do you find them repulsive?"

She cocked her head to one side. "Are you fishing for compliments? No. Of course, not. They are a part of you and you are a handsome man with a beautiful body."

"If that is true, why do you find it so hard to accept that I find you beautiful. Your scars are just another part of you. A part that is very important to me because it means you survived, you fought and you came to me."

He pulled her body close to his. She felt his arousal pressing against her stomach. "I want you, Ella. You arouse me as no woman ever has."

She turned her face up to him. "Truly?"

"Truly," he said just before his lips claimed hers in a searing kiss she felt all the way to her toes.

Her arms came up around his neck and she pressed herself more fully against him.

He broke the kiss and rested his forehead against hers. "You are my wife. *Mine*. That makes you the most desirable woman in the world to me."

She smiled, suddenly feeling all warm inside. He wanted her. Her. As she was.

*****

Daniel Adams followed Ella all the way to Golden City in the Colorado Territory. He hadn't been able to get near to Joshua. His bodyguards were good at their jobs, but Ella…she'd left the city. She was trying to get away from him, though she couldn't know that.

Their father had been very good at keeping Daniel a secret. He didn't want his *legitimate* children to know he'd been unfaithful to their mother. Daniel was the oldest of Robert Davenport's children, but Robert hadn't been married to Daniel's mother. She was his mistress. Daniel wouldn't inherit anything. Robert saw to his upbringing and that was all. He didn't figure he owed Daniel anything else. He was wrong. He owed Daniel everything and he was going to pay. Well, his children would pay now. Robert already paid with his life. Now it was time for Ella to pay with hers.

*****

Ella woke to the most delicious sensations. Her breast was alive. Sensation upon sensation traveled through her. Nathan sucked on her nipple and she couldn't help herself, she grabbed his head and held him to her. Willed him to continue the wicked things his mouth and tongue were doing to her. Continue giving her the delightful feelings that raced through her body.

He chuckled and raised his head despite her efforts to keep him to his task. "I see sleeping beauty is awake." He bent his head, licked her nipple and then blew on it. The little peak rose, craving more attention.

"Nathan," she said, her voice a mere whisper of breath.

He smiled and gave her a quick kiss on the

lips. "Come on sleepy head, time to get up and get dressed."

It was morning, yet it was still black outside. "It's still night," she complained.

"It's morning. The men and I start work as soon as the sun is up, so breakfast comes before that and you're cooking, or at least helping Martha. I'd like for you to learn and take over all the cooking. Martha deserves to have some time off."

"Of course." She nodded and yawned.

"Get up and let's see your sores." He stood up, still naked as the day he was born.

Ella looked, stared, at his naked beauty before she looked up and saw his grin.

He crossed his arms over his chest. "I'm very glad you like what you see. It is most gratifying."

She closed her eyes and got up off her side of the bed. "It's just new to me. I'm sure if I saw more naked men I would find you less fascinating."

He fell onto the bed and grabbing her nightgown, pulled her down to the bed with him.

She squealed.

"There will not be any seeing other men naked. You are stuck with this one."

She started laughing.

He smiled and then laughed with her.

"I'm glad to see I can rouse some jealousy from you, husband." Then she reached up and touched his cheek. "I want no other man."

He bent his head and kissed her, first tenderly and then completely. "Good, because you'll get no other. Now get up I want to see how your sores are this morning."

She stood up. "They must be better, I don't feel them."

"Well. What are you waiting for?"

"I'm not used to undressing in front of anyone, much less a man."

"How did you get your dresses made if you didn't undress to get them fitted?"

"I made them myself."

He raised his eyebrows "You sew that well?"

"I said I was going to make you a shirt."

"Yes, and I was prepared to like it, though I figured the effort would be pitiful."

She put her hands on her hips. "How dare you? My efforts are not pitiful. I make all my own clothes."

"I can see that you're a fine seamstress, so if you don't take that nightgown off and I rip it off you, you can make yourself another one."

She backed up clutching the neck of her gown to her. "You wouldn't dare."

He stalked her around the bed. "Wouldn't I."

"All right, all right, here," she whipped the offending gown over her head.

Nathan came around the bed, clearly ready to make love to her. She closed her eyes.

She was unprepared for the gentleness with which he touched her. Lifted her breasts so he could see underneath them, turned her around so he could see her back.

"They're better. The salve is working its

magic. Get dressed and don't even think of putting on that corset or the one I found in the drawer last night. I will destroy them if you make me."

She marched in all her naked glory to the bureau and yanked open the drawer with her bloomers and chemises in it. Grabbing one of each she put the chemise on then took a pair of stockings from another drawer and rolled one up her leg. Only then did she notice Nathan, watching her, hunger in his eyes and on his face and lower...she could tell he liked watching. She decided to tease him a bit. She rolled the second stocking slowly up, watching his eyes darken. Then suddenly he was there. Punishing her with his lips.

"You shouldn't tease a man who wants you as much as I do. It's not nice." Then he pushed her back on to the bed and came down upon her.

"Nathan?" She was as breathless as he was. "Nathan! Don't. Not like this. Not yet."

He stilled. His breathing rough. "You're right. Forgive me."

"No," she shook her head. "It is you who

must forgive me. I shouldn't have teased you if I wasn't prepared for the consequences. When next I tease you, it will be with full awareness and desire."

She put her bloomers on and then went to the closet, grabbed a shirt and black skirt to wear with it. She jammed her arms into the blouse, buttoned it up and put on the skirt.

"Feel better?" Nathan said from the bed where he laid naked, his arms behind his head.

"Much, actually. It's rather freeing not to wear a corset. I can actually bend over to put my shoes on. I haven't been able to do that in years. Now rather than lying there with a…grin on your face you need to get ready, too."

He yawned and rolled over, his back to her. "I think I'll sleep for a while longer now that you're up."

"Oh, no you don't," she slapped his naked butt, the sound reverberating in the silence. "You get your handsome butt out of bed."

He laughed, the sound delicious to her ears. "Alright, if you put it that way."

Still chuckling he got dressed and they walked down to the kitchen together.

Martha was already busy with breakfast, rolling out the biscuit dough. "Ah, there you two are. I was beginning to wonder if you'd be down at all for breakfast."

Ella blushed and looked at Nathan to find he had a big grin on his face. It seemed everything was sexual with him and it all tickled him.

"What do you want me to do first?" asked Ella.

"You can cut out these biscuits and get them ready for the oven. Cut out as many as you can, then take the leftover dough put it back into a ball and roll it out again. Flour the rolling pin so it doesn't stick to the dough. Keep doing that until you only got enough dough for one biscuit left."

"I can do that."

"I'll leave you ladies to it. I'm milking the cows this morning, but tomorrow, Ella's learning how to do it."

"Oh, I'd like that. I'm eager to learn."

Nathan leaned down and whispered in her ear, "And I've got a lot to teach you." Then he flicked his tongue against her ear.

"Oh!" She touched her hand to her ear then grabbed the rolling pin. "You better leave now before I take this rolling pin and use it on you instead of the dough."

He raised his hands in defense. "I'm leaving, I'm leaving."

His laughter followed him out of the kitchen.

"Sounds like you and my Nathan are gettin' on good. I'm glad to hear it. He's needed someone in his life for a long time now."

"How old is he?" Ella was too embarrassed to ask him. She should have found out from Mrs. Selby, but it never crossed her mind.

Martha thought about it for a moment. "He's got to be thirty–four now."

"Ten years older than me," said Ella almost to herself.

"Guess so. Didn't think you was that old."

Indignant, she said, "I'm plenty old enough."

"Never said ya wasn't." Martha nodded toward the counter. "Better get back to that dough. The men will be in to eat in about an hour and we got a lot of cookin' to do afore that."

A lot of cooking was exactly what they did. In addition to the biscuits, Martha made scrambled eggs, bacon, sausage, beans, cornbread. There were two pies, pancakes with chokecherry syrup and lots and lots of coffee. She'd made two pots before breakfast started and as soon as the first one was finished she started on a third pot.

They carried the food to the dining room. It was a lovely room. Ella quite liked the natural wood that the room was completed with. It was masculine. It reminded her of Nathan. Strong, lean.

After all the men had filed in and were seated, Nathan introduced her. "Men, this is Ella, my new bride. I know you'll all make her feel welcome."

They replied, "Welcome Ella" or "Welcome Mrs. Ravenclaw."

She and Martha put everything on the huge dining room table and it was now laden from end to end with food. Ella had never seen anyone eat as much as these men did, including Nathan. And none of them were fat. Most of them were lean, one was even skinny. He was called Slim and he ate more than anyone.

By the time they finished and were leaving to get to work, the sun was up and Ella was already exhausted.

Martha noticed and said, "You'll get used to it. The first couple days 'll be the hardest, but I kin tell yer not a quitter."

"No, I'm not. But it may take me more than a few days to get used to it. Nonetheless, what's next? Dishes I assume."

"Yup. You wash and I'll dry and put away. You can watch where things go and then after dinner, you'll dry and put 'em away."

"Okay, let's get started."

As soon as they finished the dishes, Martha had them start making the bread for dinner. They'd let it rise while they started the housework.

"How do you get anything besides cooking done? Feeding eighteen people, sixteen of them hard working men, takes a lot of food. I noticed you keep beans on the stove all the time."

"I want 'em to have something to eat whenever they're hungry. They work too hard to go without food when they need it."

"I agree. So what do we do when we're not cooking?"

"Today we change the linens and dust. There's not time for much more'n that."

"I do know how to change a bed. I always took care of my own room at home."

"Good. The clean ones are in the closet in the little bedroom. Figured it would take a while before you'd be using that bedroom," cracked Martha.

Ella felt the heat in her cheeks as she turned left the room. She got clean sheets for her and

Nathan's bed and for Martha's. The beds in the other rooms hadn't been used and she didn't see any reason to change them.

After she'd finished that, she got a dust rag from Martha and started dusting. Everything. Luckily Nathan didn't have a lot of knick-knacks to dust. Still the house was big and there were plenty of surfaces that gathered dust.

By the time she finished, it was time to fix dinner. Martha killed and plucked four chickens. Ella thought she'd be sick.

"I'm not doing that. *Ever*. Don't even bother trying to teach me. If you don't do it and Nathan wants chicken he can kill them and prepare them. I won't."

Martha laughed. "Finally some gumption from ya. I was beginning to think Nathan had his own little slave."

Ella pouted. "I don't know what you mean. I want to learn how to be a good wife to Nathan and except for the chickens, I think I'm doing well."

"Never said ya wasn't." She handed Ella a

bowl of fresh peas to shell. "Yer doin' great. But you need to know yer limits or you'll get stampeded right under."

"Stampeded? What is that?"

"A stampede is when all the cows get to runnin' in one direction. They'll run over anything or anyone who gets in their way. It's real dangerous."

Ella sat down and started shelling the peas for supper. "Does that happen very often?"

"No," said Martha as she took a seat at the table with her own pile of peas to shell. "Thank the good Lord."

CHAPTER 4

By the end of the third day, Ella was beyond exhausted. She was so tired she couldn't think straight and was questioning her decisions much less her skills. When she and Nathan got to their room all she wanted to do was fall into bed. She sat in the chair in one corner of the room and took off her shoes and stockings. Next she took off her skirt and blouse. By the time she was down to her bloomers and chemise she'd had enough and decided to sleep in them rather than wrestle with her night gown.

She lifted her arms to take down her hair

and groaned. Her arms were so sore and tomorrow was laundry day. She'd never make it. Ella wasn't a quitter, but this was so hard. She started to cry.

Nathan, who had been watching her, was suddenly there, holding her. "It's alright. I know you're tired. That's all, you're just tired. Here let me help you." She laid her head on his chest and wrapped her arms around his waist. He removed the pins from her hair and it fell around her waist. He ran his fingers through the thick sable tresses and loosened them. Then he massaged her scalp. It felt so good, she relaxed some.

"Feel better?"

"Hmm. Yes. Thank you."

He rubbed his hands up and down her arms. Then moved her hair to one side and kissed her neck. Shivers replaced the soreness of her muscles.

"Take off your chemise and bloomers."

"I…"

"I want to see how your sores are doing."

She nodded not wanting him to stop kissing her.

He helped her get off the top pulling it over her head. Then she stepped out of her bloomers. She should be embarrassed to be standing in front of him naked while he was fully clothed, but she was too tired to care.

"Beautiful," he said looking at her, his eyes dark with passion. "Turn around, let me see your back first."

She turned and he gently touched her. "They look better. I'm going to put some more salve on them."

She had to admit it felt good. Whether it was the ointment or his touch, she wasn't sure.

"Now turn around." When she did he lifted her breast to see the sores underneath. Then as he released it he ran his thumb over her nipple. She swung her gaze to his. It felt so good, sending shock waves right to the center of her womanhood.

He did it again and she moaned, "Nathan."

His lips crashed down on her. He took all that she would give and then some. She opened her mouth to him. She learned quickly and it was now as automatic as breathing. Her hands worked their way up his chest and around his neck. He crushed her to him.

Exhaustion gave way to passion. His shirt was in her way. She wanted to feel his naked skin against her own. Warmth against warmth. Flesh against flesh. She began to undo the buttons on his shirt. Frustrated she ripped one off and he ripped the others, buttons flying everywhere. She'd have to sew them back on tomorrow, but right now she didn't care.

"Nathan, please." She didn't know what she asked for only that she needed more and he could provide it.

He toed off his boots, undid his belt and dropped his drawers and pants.

She stood back and admired her husband who's manhood stood long, wide and proud.

"Come here" he commanded and she eagerly complied. He lifted her up, carried her to the bed and lowered them both to the mattress. "What do you want from me, Ella? Tell me."

"I…I don't know."

"Do you want this?" He kissed her neck.

"Yes."

"And this?" He licked where he'd kissed and then lightly blew on it, sending shivers up and down her spine.

"Yes." Her breathing came in pants now. But what she really needed was *more*. More what, she didn't know.

He moved lower and circled her nipple with his tongue and then sucked it into his mouth. He pulled back with a resounding pop. "How about that?"

"Yes." She pulled his head back down to her. "Oh, God, yes."

He chuckled. "I knew there was passion in you." He took her other nipple into his mouth and lavished it with his tongue pulling little mewling sounds from her.

"Nathan, you said you wouldn't make love to me until I asked, well I'm asking. Please, make me your wife."

"With pleasure, darlin'. With pleasure."

He moved from her breasts down her stomach to her belly button, poked his tongue in and out of it. She wasn't totally naïve. She knew he'd be making that same motion with another part of his anatomy in short order.

"I'm going to make you the happiest woman on earth. Are you ready?"

She squirmed on the bed, his hands and mouth giving her wonderful sensations that traveled direct to her lady parts. He kissed her and moved lower. As embarrassed as she was, she couldn't stop him, didn't want to stop him. She needed the completion only he could give.

The next thing she knew his mouth was on her, his tongue stabbing against her pleasure nub. She throbbed and arched off the bed, needing closer to his wonderful tongue.

"Nathan!" She wrapped her legs around him trapping his head where it was. He laughed and the vibrations nearly sent her over the edge.

"Nathan, please. Help me."

"Alright, love, alright." He slid one then two fingers into her warmth and sizzored them in and out, stretching her as he did. Then he sucked her little bud and stabbed it, flicked it with the point of his tongue.

"Oh, oh my God. Nathan!" she shouted the words as she became a star shooting through the heavens.

As she came back to earth, Nathan raised himself over her. "I'm sorry for any pain I cause you." With those words he slid his member inside her as far as he could easily, then back out and in again a little farther. She felt him against her barrier and then he backed out and slammed back into her, shoving through the barrier in one swift strike. There was some discomfort and he held himself still at her sharp intake of breath.

"Hold still, Ella. It'll be better in a moment."

"I don't want to hold still." She moved her body against his. "There's no more pain. Love me now."

He kept still only for a moment at her words. Then began to move in and out of her. She was a little awkward, but soon had the rhythm down. Back when he did and up when he pressed forward.

Soon he was moving fast, slamming against her. Fire built within her with each stroke of his penis inside her. She exploded. He followed with a roar of her name then buried his face in her neck and pumped once, twice, three times, his hot seed pouring into her.

Her heart pounded, her breathing was ragged. His was the same. She heard his rapid heartbeat beneath her ear. They laid there, her arms around his shoulders, her legs relaxed to the sides of his as they caught their breath. He rolled to the side taking her with him.

"Ella."

"Yes."

"I don't want there to be any misunderstandings between us. We are married in every sense of the word, but there is not love. There may never be."

"Because of my scars." She tried to pull away from him. He refused to let her.

"No. Not because of your scars. I simply don't believe in love. I thought myself in love once. I was shown the error of my ways by being run out of town. Never again will I put myself in that position."

"What about children? Can you love them when you don't love their mother?" She sounded whiny to her own ears, but she didn't care.

"Of course. Children are different. They are a part of me. They are innocent, their love pure. I have no doubt you will be a good mother. That's all I require. As we get to know each other, we'll form a friendship. Of that I have no doubt."

"You're lucky I want children or I'd never have sex with you again." Angry, she tried to pull away from him, but he held her fast. She was angrier than she'd ever been, though she wasn't completely sure why. Maybe it was because Nathan refused to give them a chance before they even got to know each other.

"Yes, you would. You have too much passion. But tonight is your first time and you'll be sore. Stay right there." He got up and went to the commode and poured water from the pitcher into the basin. Then he returned to her with a damp washcloth. "Let me ease your soreness. You'll feel better in the morning."

She let him clean her. He was extremely gentle. Unexpected from someone supposedly devoid of feelings.

Her heart knew her husband wasn't incapable of falling in love with her. But he was scared. Frightened of being hurt again. She understood that. She could, would work around that.

He insisted her scars didn't matter and she'd take him at his word for now. She intended to make him fall in love with her because, fortunately or not, she was afraid she'd already fallen for him.

*****

Daniel Adams spent the first two weeks of his stay at the Astor House searching for Ella. He frequented the mercantile and the other shops in town, hoping to run into her. His patience was finally rewarded when she came in with her husband, an admittedly handsome man with golden skin. Quite the contrast to Ella's exceedingly pale, white complexion.

Ella was shy, kept her right side, her good side, to the store's owner. Finally, she faced the man and he was able to see her scars. Daniel eagerly anticipated the horror on the man's face when he saw the red lines that crisscrossed her cheek and neck.

He was bitterly disappointed. The man had no reaction, as though he saw someone like Ella every day.

The owner noticed him lurking among the shelves. "Ah, Mr. Adams, come meet some of our leading citizens. Nathan and Ella Ravenclaw this is Daniel Adams. He's new to our fair city. He's from New York, too, Ella. Planning to open a law office here."

"Mr. Adams," said Nathan as he extended

his hand.

Daniel shook Nathan's proffered hand. Then he touched his hat, "Ma'am," he said to Ella.

She blushed and stepped closer to her husband. "Mr. Adams."

"What is it that you do, Mr. Ravenclaw?"

Nathan put his arm around Ella's waist and drew her closer before he answered. "I'm a rancher."

"Ah. Ranching. I admit I know absolutely nothing about that particular endeavor."

"I raise cattle for the most part."

"Sounds like hard work."

"It is. But worth the effort."

Daniel didn't like the way Nathan eyed him. Suspicion clear in his striking blue eyes.

"Excuse me Mr. Adams, but have we met before?" asked Ella her eyes narrowed as though she was searching her mind for their connection.

"I don't believe so. I would have remembered a woman as beautiful as you."

Ella blushed. "You flatter me, but thank you

just the same."

"Not at all. I only speak the truth which these gentlemen can attest to."

He'd put them on the spot, but Ravenclaw and the storekeeper simply nodded in agreement. Amazingly, they really seemed to find her beautiful.

Now was the time to leave. He didn't want to over stay his welcome.

He wondered if Ella saw the resemblance to their father? That was why he seemed familiar to her. He would use that to his advantage, as soon as he figured out how to do it.

"I must leave now, it was very good meeting you," said Daniel as he tipped his hat to the two of them.

As Ella watched the stranger walk out of the store, she said to Nathan, "I don't know what it is about that man, but he seems very familiar to me."

"Maybe you met him in New York."

She shook her head. "I don't think so. I don't believe I've ever met him before, but I believe I should know him. I'll think of it soon enough"

*****

Ella and Martha became fast friends. Being the only women on the ranch, they confided in one another.

Several weeks had gone by and they were in the kitchen fixing Sunday dinner when Ella finally broached the subject of Nathan's reluctance to believe in love.

"Why is he so dead set against it?"

Martha stopped peeling potatoes and leaned her backside against the sink. "Oh, he wasn't always. Fell real hard for the daughter of another rancher. All was well and good 'til they found out he wasn't as lily white as they were. Being half Indian makes you dirt to most white folk. So Nathan picked up stakes and moved here, cattle and all. He made sure folks here knew his background and even so, they treat him fine."

"Except women. No one would marry him."

"Right. Except for that, but I don't figure he ever would have asked anyone here anyway. He wasn't gonna take the chance that he'd have to pull up stakes again."

Ella wiped at the tears that filled her eyes.

"Now don't you go feelin' sorry for Nathan. He'd never want that. Sides I figure he done alright. He got you didn't he?"

She laughed and sniffled. "That's right and whether he knows it or not I'm the best thing that ever happened to him."

"He doesn't disagree." Nathan leaned against the door jam, arms akimbo.

"Oh, my. How much did you hear?"

"Just that you're the best thing that's happened to me." He grabbed her around the waist and gave her a smack on the lips. "Like I said, I don't disagree."

She kissed him back.

"Now that's enough of that you two. We got dinner to fix," scolded Martha.

"That's what I stopped in for. I ran into John Atwood in town and invited him, Sarah and the kids for Sunday dinner. He accepted."

"Oh, that's wonderful. I can't wait to get

my hands on that sweet baby boy of theirs," said Ella, rubbing her hands together.

"I'm sure John and Sarah will be touched to know how much you want to see them."

She swatted him with a dish towel. "You know what I mean. I want to see them, too."

Nathan laughed. She knew he loved to get her dander up. He raised his hands. "Alright, I'll quit teasing."

"Good. Because iffin' ya stay any longer I'm gonna give you a knife and get you peelin' potatoes. As it is, you kin go kill me another chicken," said Martha.

He nodded. "Okay. Be right back. Better get on a pot of water to boil."

"I know how to pluck a chicken, now go on and get."

A little while later he came back in carrying the dead chicken. Ella turned to him, saw the bloody chicken and everything went black.

*****

"Ella. Honey. Wake up."

"Nathan?" He was kneeling next to her and she was lying on the sofa in the parlor. "What happened?"

"I was going to ask you the same thing. You looked at me and fainted dead away."

"I remember now. The chicken, the blood," she sat up quickly and started to heave.

Nathan jumped back. "What the hell?"

Martha came running with a bucket. "Here you go. Smelling salts does that sometimes. But in your case I think it's something else."

Ella breathed slowly letting her stomach settle. "What else could it be?"

Martha shook her head. "Ella, how long you been here?"

"About two months."

"And in all that time, have you had your flow?"

"Well, no. I…." She swung her gaze from Martha to Nathan. He sank to his knees in front of her.

"Are we…?" he asked.

She smiled widely. "It would appear we are."

He stood up, pulled her into his arms and swung her around. "I'm going to be a father."

"Thought you two might have figured it out on your own, but...." Martha put her hands on her generous hips. "What would you do without me?"

"Martha, you're going to be a grandma. Stop your grumbling," said Ella.

Now Martha got tears in her eyes. "Me? A grandma?"

"Well, what do you expect? You're like a mother to both Nathan and me. Our baby couldn't do better for a grandma?"

Ella wrapped her arms around the older woman's shoulders and Nathan enveloped them both in his embrace.

"Boy, do we have some news to share with John and Sarah. You'll have to practice holding a baby on little Sam," said Nathan.

"Oh, I need to start sewing baby clothes. Can we go to town tomorrow and get some fabric?

I know it's not our regular day, but I don't want to wait until Saturday."

He grinned. "What's one more trip to town?"

"You could always teach me to drive and then I wouldn't have to take you away from your work when I want to go somewhere. And I'd be able to go see Sarah more often and…."

"Stop." He rolled his eyes and said, "alright I'll teach you to drive a team."

She hugged him around the waist. "Thank you. While you're at it you could teach me to ride, too."

"Not on your life. Not with you expecting."

"But Nathan I should be able to get around on my own."

"You'll have the buggy as well as the buckboard that you can drive as soon as I teach you. That's enough. I'm not going to let anything happen to you."

Ella was thrilled to be pregnant. She wanted children more than anything, but a little part of her wondered if Nathan would be so protective if she wasn't carrying his child. She put the thought aside refusing to let anything mar this moment for her.

Later that night when she and Nathan were alone in their bedroom, he made love to her with a tenderness he hadn't before. After they were done and catching their breath he leaned up on one elbow and put his other hand on her stomach making lazy circles on it.

"Our child rests here. You don't show yet."

"I will soon enough. I'll get as big as a house. Will you still want me when I look like one of your cows?"

"I will always desire you. You're my wife. You carrying my child only makes you more beautiful to me.

"I'm glad." She covered his hand with hers and wished he could, would give her more. Her feelings were as hidden as she could make them. The last thing she wanted was for him to care for her out of pity. Thus far she'd been successful. She gave all she could without letting him know, without saying it out loud, without telling him he held her heart in his hands.

He suddenly bent down and kissed her. "Thank you."

She cocked her head to one side. "For what?"

"For giving me a child."

She placed her hand along his strong jaw. "You're welcome. I thank you for the same thing. I've wanted a child of my own for as long as I can remember."

"As have I. It's the reason I married. It was one of the requirements that I made of Mrs. Selby. The woman had to be of childbearing age. A woman, not a girl just out of the schoolroom. I wanted to be able to talk to her, not raise her. I'd say she did rather well."

He leaned down and took one dusky rose nipple into his mouth. "I think she did very well." He moved to the other one. "Very well indeed."

She arched into him, her breath coming in gasps as his lips caused her core to heat. Grasping his head to her she said, "I can't say I have any complaints either."

He worked his way down her body and back up again. As always she was ready for him and he entered her in one long, smooth stroke. And so it began and she loved him all over again. Though she never referred to it as making love to him. But that's what it was. She made love to Nathan and some day he would realize that's what he did as well. He was one stubborn man. But she was even more stubborn and...patient. She could wait.

CHAPTER 5

Ella wouldn't let Nathan out of the house until he agreed to give her a driving lesson that morning before he got involved in doing other things. She cajoled and bothered him until he gave in.

He went to get the buggy while she got her gloves and bonnet. She didn't bother with the veil anymore. Most of the merchants knew her and didn't flinch when she came in. The only friends close enough to see very often were the Atwoods and they accepted her without question. Any wife of Nathan's was a friend of theirs. She and Sarah Atwood had become close friends, bonding over the

112

fact they were both from New York and had become mail order brides. Something neither could have imagined in their wildest dreams.

She left the house and ran out through the courtyard to the yard beyond and waited for him to drive up, which wasn't long. He drove up in the little two seat buggy pulled by two beautiful pinto horses.

Ella was so thrilled; she didn't wait for Nathan to help her into the seat, but climbed aboard on her own.

"You better simmer down, missy. You're going to spook the horses with all this enthusiasm."

She laughed. "I'm just excited. I can't wait to learn and be able to go around on my own."

"Tired of my company already?" he teased.

"No. I just need to have a modicum of freedom. This will allow me that. I can go see Sarah when I want, they're only about thirty minutes away or I can go to town when I need something before Saturday. It's hard. Sometimes I feel so isolated. In New York I walked everywhere.

Admittedly, not so much since the accident, but before that. And now that I don't wear the veil anymore, I'm ready to get out and start socializing again. I'm not afraid of what people will think of me. That's thanks to you. Does that make sense?"

"Yes, it does. I should have thought of it sooner. I guess I was trying to keep you all to myself."

"That's sweet, but unnecessary. I don't plan on going anywhere but to town and to Sarah's."

"I know. It's something I have to get over."

She laid her hand over his. "Just because I can drive myself doesn't mean we can't still go together. It simply means you're not forced to go with me."

"Exactly. So let's get this lesson started. Since you don't ride, and don't think I've changed my mind about that, I haven't. Anyway this will be totally unfamiliar to you. These are called the reins." He showed her the reins in his hand. "They are what guide the horses. Tells them to go forward, right, left or stop."

"Reins. Guide horses. Got it."

"To get the horses going slap them on the butt, like this. Giddyup." He brought the leather straps down on the horses butts. They started forward. "If you want them to go faster, flick them again." He showed her.

"What if I want them to go left?"

"Then you pull back on the left rein. To go right pull back on the right rein and to stop pull back on them both. You have a brake," he showed her the hand brake to his left next to the seat. "But it's just for when you're already stopped to remind the horses they aren't supposed to go anywhere. It won't stop the buggy if they are of a mind to pull it."

"Hold on tight to the reins. Don't give the horses their heads. They'll run away home if you give them the opportunity."

"What happens if they do that? How do I stop them?"

"You pull back on the reins for all you're worth, but if they spook and run you probably won't

115

be able to stop them."

"So what? I just hang on and hope for the best?" She shook her head. "What would you do?"

"If I can't get control and I can see a crash coming I'd probably jump for it."

"Wouldn't that be as bad as crashing?"

"Not necessarily. You wouldn't get tangled in with the buggy if you jump before it crashes. But I don't want you even thinking about that. You're not going to give the horses free rein. Ever. And you won't be going fast. Ever." He took off his hat and ran his fingers through his hair. "God, you've got me terrified to teach you."

She grasped his knee until he looked at her. "Nathan, I'll be fine. This isn't a carriage, so it doesn't scare me. And I'll be careful."

"There's just so much that can go wrong."

"Not with you teaching me. I'll learn to do this the right way from the beginning. I don't have any bad habits to break."

He bit his lower lip and then took a deep breath. "Okay. Here are the reins. Do you remember what to do?"

"Flick them on the horses behinds like this." She slapped the straps down. There was a good 'snap' and the horses started walking.

She grinned at her husband. "Look, I did it. They're moving."

Nathan hugged her to him. "You did it. Now let's get them moving a little faster so we can get to John and Sarah's before tomorrow. Slap the reins a little harder this time and say 'giddyup'."

"Giddyup? You said that before. What's it mean?"

"They understand. It means go faster to them."

She slapped the horses hard on their rumps and they started to trot. The gait was very jerky even though they were in the buggy, so she slapped them again. They started to canter and now the buggy was really moving. At this rate they'd be to John and Sarah's in no time.

They were moving along at a good clip when suddenly the horses shied, turned and began to gallop through the pasture next to the road. Out of control.

Ella tried to slow them. She pulled back on the reins for all she was worth. It wasn't enough. Then Nathan was there. His big hands took the reins from her and he pulled back on them. The horses slowed and came to a stop.

Nathan set the brake and took her into his arms.

Her tears fell in earnest. "I couldn't stop them. They didn't respond to me. If you hadn't been…."

"Sshh. Hush now. It's alright. I was here. They just got spooked. It happens sometimes."

"What could have spooked them? I didn't see anything."

"Probably a rattler. We have a lot of them in this country."

"Rattlers?"

"Snakes. Rattle snake. They're poisonous and have rattles on the end of their tail they use to warn people and animals that they're around. The horses probably heard one or saw one and took off."

She leaned into him. "I want to go home. I've had enough of a lesson today."

"Do you want to drive?" He held the reins up for her to take.

She shook her head. "No." She shied away from them.

He got them turned around and headed back in the direction of their house.

When they pulled up to the hitching rail in the front yard, Ella wanted to jump down and run into the house before Nathan could help her. Before he could see what a coward she was. She didn't want him to see the fear in her eyes. But she couldn't get her legs to work.

Nathan set the brake, hopped out and came around to her side. He held his hand up to her. She took it and turned on the seat, but that's as far as she could get.

"Ella. Oh baby, it's alright. Come here." He reached up and grasped her around the waist and lifted her down.

CYNTHIA WOOLF

Once on her feet her knees buckled. Nathan caught her, picked her up and carried her inside to their bedroom where he set her down on the side of the bed. He sat down beside her and put his arm around her.

She burst into tears, grabbed him around the waist and buried her face in his chest.

He wrapped his arms around her and let her cry. Didn't tell her to hush or that it would be alright, just let her cry.

"I'm sorry. I…it…it was like being in the carriage all over again. I couldn't stop what was happening. I could see it, knew we were in trouble, but couldn't stop it." She sniffled and reached for the handkerchief in her sleeve. She dabbed at her eyes and blew her nose.

"This isn't something that you have to do, not now, not ever if you don't want. Why don't you just lie down for awhile? I'll go get the horses and put them away, then come back and check on you."

She nodded and lay down on the bed.

Once Nathan left the room she allowed

herself to cry again, to relive the hell that had been relegated to her nightmares. So real. It was back and it was so real. The terror. The pain.

She curled into herself and fell asleep.

When Nathan came back he found her that way, sound asleep. He knew from prior experience that she was reliving her accident. He lay down next to her and gathered her into his arms. She went willingly and molded to his body. He held her, felt her relax and breathe easier. She'd been frightened out of her mind today. But she handled it. Didn't fall apart until they got to the house and even then she didn't turn into a screaming ninny.

He was proud of her. Considering the severity of the original accident, that she would even consider driving the buggy had been a big step forward. He didn't know if he'd get her back in it, but he thought she would. She was stronger than she thought she was, his little bride.

Ella awoke feeling warm and relaxed. Her head was pillowed on Nathan's chest and his arms held her in a circle of warmth. She was loathe to leave his embrace, but nature called. She moved his arm down so she could get up, but it came back to her breast. She gave a small gasp at the intimate contact, turned and looked up into his blue eyes, smoldering with passion.

"Hello," she said.

"Hello to you."

Now both of his hands were busy with her breasts and she almost changed her mind about getting out of bed, but her body reminded her she needed to void.

"I have to get up. Now."

"Only if you promise to come back to bed."

"I promise."

"Without your clothes."

She nodded and he released her.

Staying behind the screen, she got out of her wrinkled clothes and, out of habit, arranged her hair carefully over her left side, hiding her scars. She went out into the room and ran for the bed.

"Stop. Don't run," he commanded.

She stopped and walked the rest of the way.

Thinking to tease him she got in on his side of the bed, crawling over his naked body. He'd lost the covers, and his clothes, after she'd gotten up. He stopped her when she was fully on top of him, trapping her legs between his and allowing her to feel every aroused inch of him.

"Now that is the best idea you've had." He pulled her up until he could kiss her. And kiss her he did, gently, thoroughly, leaving her no doubt that he wanted her.

"Nathan," she breathed when he let her up. "Make love to me."

"Thought you'd never ask."

He rolled them until he was on top of her. Leaning down he nipped at her neck and then soothed with his tongue. Came back to her mouth and gave her a kiss before moving to the other side of her neck and down, down to her breast where he took one aching nipple into his mouth.

He moved her hair and she stiffened.

"Don't hide yourself from me." He kissed all along her scars, easing her, and then moved down to her other breast. "You are beautiful. All of you."

She could almost believe him. He treated her body reverently like he really cared. There was no reticence, no hesitation, he kissed every part of her, then parted her legs and kissed her there, where she ached.

"Nathan. Please."

He chuckled, but the next thing she knew his tongue was making her ache for more. Around and around her pleasure nub it went and then he sucked and licked again. The ache built until finally he sent her into oblivion, soaring among the stars.

As she started to return to earth, he drove home, her body slick and ready to receive him.

He lifted his head from her shoulder and smiled down at her. He pumped slowly. Each stroke rebuilding the fire in her. His eyes never left hers as she began to move with him, up when he pushed in and back when he pulled out. Each stroke buried him deeper and deeper until he touched her womb. He picked up that pace and she began to build toward that wonderful pinnacle she'd fallen off of before.

Nathan thrust twice more, reached between them and said, "Come with me, Ella," as he touched her nubbin sending her over the precipice. She heard him groan and then he buried his face in her neck, among her scars and she didn't care. This was right and so wonderful.

He lay heavy upon her, still inside her and then he rolled taking her with him, throwing one leg over hers, he pulled her close.

These were the moments she loved. Having him hold her after they made love could almost make her believe he loved her. Almost. She had to remind herself not to fall in love with him. He couldn't love her back. Handsome men like him didn't fall in love with women like her. She was heir to a fortune, but men only wanted the money, not her. But, a little voice reminded her, Nathan doesn't know you're rich. You've never told him. Maybe you should. It's his money now, too.

"Nathan."

"Hmm."

"Don't go to sleep yet. We need to talk."

He hugged her close. "What about?"

"Us."

She felt him tense up. "What about us?"

"I'm rich."

He relaxed. "So am I. I have you."

She sighed. He wasn't going to make this easy. "No. Really. I'm rich. My brother and I inherited my father's shipyard when he was killed."

"That's nice."

"It doesn't bother you?"

"Why should it? Every man wants a rich wife. Besides," he gave her a hug. "I'm wealthy on my own and I'll inherit from my father one day. He's a very rich man. The fact that you have money means nothing to me. Keep it or spend it, as you please."

"You really don't care?" she hugged him and rubbed her hand over his smooth chest. "Since I can spend it, you just said I could, I want to hire someone to put a bathroom and running water in the house."

"I can pay for that," he grumbled.

"I know, but so can I. Please let me do this. For us. For our children."

"For the children?" He cocked an eyebrow.

"Yes, it will be ever so much easier to keep the little ones clean with running water in the house and a bathroom with a big tub in it. Maybe one big enough for the two of us together." She winked at him.

"Are you flirting with me in order to get your way?"

She laughed. "Yes. Is it working? Can I hire a plumber to come put water in the house?"

"I suppose so. Will that make you happy?"

"Ecstatic."

"Good. Now let's go to sleep. Morning comes early and you've already kept me up with your incessant demands to make love."

"Me?! It was you—"

He chuckled.

She shook her head. "You love to get me all

riled up."

"Well, you *are* easy to rile. It's fun to watch."

"I'm going to stop taking anything you say seriously."

He rolled her until she lay atop him. "I'm very serious when I say I want you." He pushed his pelvis up so she was sure of his erection. "But if I take you again, we won't get any sleep. So," he rolled to his side, "close your beautiful brown eyes and go to sleep." He turned over and blew out the lamp.

She was much too excited to sleep. Her mind raced and she thought of babies. Touching her still flat stomach she wondered if her children would have their father's dark good looks or her pale skin? It didn't matter who her babies took after, they were already loved.

Or might they take after her father with his golden blond coloring. That was who Joshua favored. He had blond hair and bronzed skin from working in the shipyard. At least he had until their father was murdered. Now he worked in the office as her father had. Joshua still kept his hand in the actual building of the ships. It's what he loved. He worked one day a week in the yard and the rest of the time in the office. It was enough to keep his skin sun kissed.

Thinking about Joshua made her a little homesick. Would she be able to see him again? Would Nathan want to go to New York? Could he even spend that much time away from the ranch? She knew she didn't want to make the trip alone. The trip had been bad enough alone the first time.

What about when she had the child? Could Joshua come there? He surely could leave the business for a time. Benjamin, his assistant, could handle it and they had a telegraph in Golden City, if Joshua's input was really necessary.

Finally, she decided she'd have Nathan take her to town so she could telegraph Joshua. Just making the decision relaxed her and she rolled over to go to sleep. Nathan's arms still held her loosely. She rolled out of them and to her side. Even in his sleep he reached for her and laid one arm over her. Very possessive, her husband, yet he understood her need to be independent, too. He wanted her to learn to drive the buggy and she wanted to. She was afraid, but she would overcome her fear by facing it. She had the basics of driving and she would face her fear head on. Tomorrow. She'd think about it tomorrow. That would be soon enough, she thought as sleep overtook her.

*****

She kicked at the irritant. Something tickled her feet.

"Wake up, sleepy head." His deep voice rolled over her and she felt just delicious.

She sighed. "Is is morning already?"

"Yup and you've got breakfast to make. Martha has already got the coffee going and is gathering the eggs as we speak. So get your beautiful ass out of bed." He swatted said ass.

"Ow. All right. I'm up. I'm up." She kicked off the covers and sat up. Thank goodness she'd gotten a nap yesterday because she didn't get much sleep last night. The thought made her smile.

"What are you thinking about?"

"Nothing."

He chuckled. "Well, *nothing* has you blushing right down to your toes. And *nothing* is going to happen again tonight."

She was sure her cheeks and other naked parts were flaming. She grabbed the first thing she found, a black bombazine dress. Much too heavy for the work she had to to today, she hung it back in the closet and traded it for a light cotton dress in red with small white flowers. It was quite fitted showing off her figure.

Nathan gave her a wicked smile and said, "You look good enough to eat, but I'll wait until tonight."

"You have to stop saying those things; I'm in a perpetual state of embarrassment."

"It becomes you." He gave her a quick kiss and headed out to start his morning chores. There were horses, pigs and milk cows to be fed.

She finished dressing and doing her morning

ablutions and then went to the kitchen. There she put three big cast iron skillets on the stove filled with bacon and sausage. After that she poured herself a cup of the coffee Martha made and started on the first batch of biscuits. Feeding fifteen hungry cowboys was a lot of work and when that was done there was still housework to do.

Except for some light cooking all of these were things she'd never done until now. She'd had maids and cooks for all of her twenty-four years. Her old nursemaid, Bridget, had taken care of her after the accident. That had been the hardest thing to do, saying goodbye to Bridget.

She'd thought of bringing her along, but didn't want to subject the elderly woman to the hardships of the trip. It was for the best all around. Bridget would have tried to do all the work and Ella would have learned nothing.

In these last two months, her whole life had changed. She had a husband, a home of her own, not her father's or her brother's, but hers. She was going to have a baby soon, well in seven months, but that was soon enough. She'd have someone she could love unconditionally and who would love her back. Maybe when she gave Nathan a child he would fall in love with her, too. She knew she'd already fallen in love with her husband. He was strong yet kind and intelligent. He treated her gently. A powerful combination. He was all man. The best kind of man.

CHAPTER 6

Laundry day. The worst day of the week as far as Ella was concerned. She hated standing over the wash tub and stirring the clothes in boiling water with the long wooden paddle. Even when the water got cool enough for her to put her hands in, the harsh lye soap still ate at them. They were no longer the lily white, soft appendages she'd arrived in Golden City with. Now, more often than not, they were red and chapped and sometimes hurt like hell.

She chastised herself for her language. That was another thing she'd learned. How to cuss. Martha was good at it, her language often very colorful. Nathan tended to watch his language in front of her, but she heard him, when he didn't think she could hear, cuss a blue streak more than once. Usually over something that one of the cowboys did. He never disciplined them in front of the other men, but they heard about whatever it was in private.

Laundry was almost done. All she had to do was hang it. She put it in the basket and carried it to the clothes line. She started to put the basket down when she saw it. A snake coiled right in front of her. She stopped, but not soon enough. It struck and caught her on the leg above her ankle.

She dropped the laundry basket. It landed on the snake, blocking it from striking again. "Nathan!"

Martha heard her and came running. "What in the world is wrong?"

Ella walked to her. "I got bit by a snake. Get Nathan. Hurry."

She sat down on the porch steps and waited for what seemed like an eternity. Knowing that with every heartbeat the poison pushed its deadly way through her system. Her leg hurt like the dickens.

Nathan came running with Martha far behind. His long legs ate up the distance between the barn and the house.

"Ella. Honey. Show me the bite."

She lifted her dress. There were two distinct marks on her leg.

"We have to get the poison out." He took his knife and cut across the two bites. Then he put his mouth on her and sucked. He spit the blood out and repeated the procedure. "I know that some of the poison is still in your system, but you're going to be fine."

Ella nodded. "I don't feel well, Nathan. I'm scared."

He picked her up and carried her to the bedroom. There he undressed her and put her in her nightgown. "I'll get you some water. I sent one of the boys for the doctor."

Ella closed her eyes and the tears began to

fall. "I'm going to die aren't I?"

"No. You're not. Snake bites aren't usually fatal, but you're going to be very sick for awhile. I'll get you some water. You just lie here and rest."

"Nathan. I don't want to die. What about the baby?"

"I don't know. I just don't know, Ella." He sat on the bed and took her in his arms.

She cried harder clutching his shirt, holding him to her. "I can't lose the baby. Oh, God, please don't let me lose this baby."

"We'll get through this no matter what happens. I think I hear a buggy. That's probably the doc. You just lie here for a bit. I'll be right back."

The tears fell faster after Nathan left and she was still crying when the doctor came in the room.

"Mrs. Ravenclaw, you must calm down. I'm going to give you a little bit of laudanum. I want you to drink it all down," said the doctor.

Knowing she needed to relax and still unable to, she did as she was told.

"Did you kill the snake? I dropped the laundry basket on it. It's probably still trapped." She grabbed Nathan's shirt. "You have to go kill it. I want to know it's dead."

"All right." He unwound her hands from the front of his shirt. "I'll go do that now while the doctor is here and can watch you. Now just relax and let the medicine take effect."

She lay back and tried to calm herself. Tried to slow her racing heart. It was a lost cause. Worry for the baby made her cry again. "I can't stop worrying about my baby," she told the doctor.

"We'll cross that bridge when we come to it, but the most help you can give that little one is to calm yourself."

A few minutes later Nathan came back in the room. He smiled at her and the doctor. "Well, I killed the snake you trapped with the basket. It wasn't a rattler. Just a bull snake. An easy mistake to make. They look alike, but the bull snake doesn't have the rattles…or the venom. You're going to be fine."

Ella burst into tears. Tears of relief.

Nathan came over and took her in his arms. "Shh. It's okay."

She shook her head. "I thought I was going to die, that our baby would die. I'm an idiot and my leg hurts."

The doctor said, "I'll clean the wound on your leg and bandage it. You've had quite a scare today and I'd like for you to remain in bed for the rest of the day and just relax. Let's get you to feeling better and let that baby rest up from this scare, too."

She sniffled and shook her head. "I still have to hang the laundry."

"Martha will hang the clothes. She's already started. You just relax." Nathan put his hand on her tummy. "He needs you to."

The doctor cleaned and wrapped Ella's leg. He gave instructions for the bandage to be changed in the morning and every two days until it was healed.

"Even with a non-venomous bite, it's still

painful and can easily get infected. You need to keep it clean and dry."

"I'll see to it," said Nathan. "Nothing's going to happen to her."

It almost sounded like he loved her. Ella was thrilled at the prospect then realized he was probably worried about the baby, not her.

Ella spent the rest of the day in bed. She didn't know if it was the laudanum the doctor gave her or just the relief at not harming the baby, but she was tired. The stresses of the past hour were catching up to her. Her eyelids felt like they were made of lead and she let them fall closed.

Nathan came in with Ella's supper tray. He'd checked on her several times during the day and each time she'd been asleep. Now though he decided she needed to eat more than she needed more sleep. She was never going to rest tonight if she didn't wake up now. He put the tray on the top of the dresser and sat on the edge of the bed.

"Ella. Honey." He ran his hand up her arm and back down again. "Wake up. You need to eat supper."

She opened her eyes, blinking several times. "It's time for supper? I lost the whole day," she lamented.

"You needed the rest." He'd worried when she'd slept so much, but convinced himself she was all right. "How's your leg? Does it still hurt?"

She thought about it for a moment. "No, actually it is better. You didn't need to bring me supper. I could've come to the kitchen."

"You're fine where you are. Tomorrow will be soon enough for you to be up and around again."

She sat up and smiled at him. "Tomorrow! The Atwoods are coming for dinner." She stopped and closed her eyes willing herself to calm. "I am kind of hungry though. Thank you for the tray."

He put the tray on her lap. She picked up her fork and dug into the mashed potatoes. He'd tried not to give her too much food, it looked like about half what he would eat. It was still more than she wanted.

"Did you get enough? You didn't eat very

much."

"I got plenty." She smiled at him. "*Your* eyes were bigger than *my* stomach."

He chuckled. "Well, I guess the dog will be eating good tonight."

"Are you coming to bed soon?"

"Probably. I've got some paperwork to do first. Do you want me to get you a book to read?"

"I can come get one. I need to get up. I've been in bed all day. I need to move." She sat up on the side of the bed. "See no problem."

"Let me walk with you…just in case."

Sarah shook her head. "If you want, but there is really no need. It was just a little bite. Something a real western wife would just ignore and go back to work."

"Whoa." Nathan grabbed her by the shoulder and brought her to a halt. "What do you mean a real western wife? Ella you are my wife and you are doing great and learning at an alarming rate. You're willing to try anything and you're a quick study, getting "it" the first time. Don't ever let me hear you disparaging yourself again."

Sarah looked up into his face. He meant every word.

*****

John and Sarah Atwood arrived with their children right at noon. It was perfect timing. Dinner would be served at one o'clock so there'd be time to visit before and after the meal.

Their two little girls, Katy and MaryAnn played with their baby brother, Samuel, on the parlor floor while their parents visited. Nathan and John went to Nathan's office to discuss cattle and Sarah went to the kitchen with Ella to help with meal preparations.

"Alright, ladies," said Ella to Sarah and Martha. "I need some advice."

"What can we help you with?" asked Sarah.

"Well, Nathan and I get along pretty well, I think, but I want more. More than just a friendship. More than just his passion. I want his love."

Sarah and Martha looked at each other and burst into laughter.

Ella put her hands on her hips. "What's so funny?"

"You are," said Sarah, once she finished laughing. She went over to Ella and put her arm around her shoulder. "Nathan is already in love with you. Don't you see it? The way he looks at you? Touches you?"

"No. He looks at me with passion in his eyes and he's gentle with me because of the baby."

"So," said Martha. "He was harsh with you before the baby? He treated you badly?"

"No, of course, not. He's always been gentle and kind with me. Almost too much so. I keep telling him that I'm not breakable."

"Does he always find a reason to touch you? Kiss you? Does he take off just to spend time with you? Does he hold you after you make love or fall right to sleep?"

Ella slumped down in the wooden chair at the end of the long oak table, her mind a whirl. Was it possible? When they'd first started making love he held her for a short time then turned his back to her and went to sleep. Now he held her in his arms all night. And he always managed to take the time from his work to take her to town when she needed something even though Martha could have done it easier.

"He loves me," she said finally.

"He loves you," said Sarah and Martha simultaneously.

"He has for some time," continued Martha. "I noticed the change. I've seen the way he looks at you when he thinks no one is watching. The longing there, the joy when you enter a room. If you'd just stop worrying about it, you'd see it, too."

"Getting him to admit it…well that's not so easy," said Sarah. "I remember John wouldn't admit it until I almost died. Let's hope it doesn't take that long for Nathan."

"I don't know," said Martha. "My Nathan's head is as hard as John's. After what happened with Hettie, I can't blame him for being skittish as a new born colt."

Ella got up and started putting the food on

platters and in serving bowls. She needed to keep
her hands busy. Today she'd fixed several big pot
roasts brimming with carrots, onions and potatoes.
She put everything onto separate plates for serving.
Then took the roasts and broke them apart with two
forks. They shredded beautifully and Ella couldn't
help but feel some pride in her dish.

"Hettie. Is that the woman he was going to
marry until she found out he was part Indian?"
asked Ella.

"Yup, that's her. A more selfish woman
you'd never want to meet. She cared about
Nathan's money, not Nathan."

"I'm not interested in Nathan's money."

"I know. You married him not knowing if
he had two nickels to rub together."

"I'm not as altruistic as you may think. It
just never occurred to me to wonder whether he had
any money." She shrugged her shoulders. "I have
money of my own."

Martha chortled. "Well what do you know?
Nathan's the one who married money."

"Back to the problem at hand. How do I get him to realize he loves me? Or do I just leave it as it is?" She shook her head. "No, I want him to tell me he loves me. I need for him to know it as deeply as I know I love him."

"I wish I knew what to tell you," said Sarah.

They both looked to Martha for an answer.

"Don't look at me. Sure, I've known him the longest, but I've never seen him like this before. You know as much as I do."

"He'll realize it when the baby is born. John said birthing the baby terrified him more than when I was shot because there was nothing he could do to help me."

"I don't know, " said Martha. "Nathan came home after that and said he couldn't understand why John was so anxious. That Arapaho women do it all the time without making a sound."

"Ha! I don't believe it. I screamed my head off or tried to."

Ella swallowed hard. "Screamed?"

Sarah looked at her and her whole demeanor

changed to one of sympathy. "Oh, Ella, it is the most wondrous thing, but I won't lie to you. Birthing a babe is the hardest, most painful thing you'll ever do. But once you get that baby in your arms, well," she got a far off look in her eyes. "None of the other matters. You don't remember the pain, just the sweet face of the beautiful little person you've created. Who now depends on you and loves you and who you love more than anything in this life."

Ella couldn't get past the pain part. She was not one to tolerate pain easily. Headaches nearly sent her to her bed for gosh sakes. She sat at the table, weak in the knees. "Pain? How much pain did you say?"

Sarah came over and put her arm around Ella's shoulders. "Oh, honey, don't worry about it. I didn't mean to scare you. It'll be fine and you won't regret any of it. Honest."

"Would you do it again?"

"In a heartbeat." Sarah smiled. "I'm hoping that we'll have another one soon. I want to have lots of children. I don't know what I'd do without my Katy, MaryAnn and Sam. They are my life, next to John."

Ella took a deep breath and rose from the chair. "Well, I never thought any of this would be easy, so I guess I just better get on with it."

"Get on with what?" asked Nathan, his deep baritone voice washing over her like silk.

"On with dinner," said Ella quickly. "Before it all gets cold. Martha would you call the men please?"

Nathan looked at her and cocked his head, narrowed his eyes in question and then frowned.

Ella shook her head at him and went about making sure all the food was on the table. Because there were so many of them to eat today, she had all the food on the kitchen table and counters. Each person filed by filling their plates before going to the dining room to be seated. Once all the men had taken their fill, Ella had the children go next, followed by the Atwoods, Martha, her and Nathan. There was plenty to go around so no worries that they would run out of anything.

Dinner around the huge dark cherry wood table turned into a boisterous affair with the men talking about the new Hereford cows Nathan got and the bull that John bought in Kansas City and had shipped in. It still galled her that cattle could ride the train all the way to Golden City, but people couldn't.

The little girls were busy telling Martha stories and Sarah had Sam and was feeding him mashed potatoes and carrots. The little tyke seemed to enjoy them, only spitting out about half of each bite.

Ella was surrounded by people and felt utterly alone. Tears began to pool in her eyes.

"Excuse me," she said and got up from the table as quickly as she could before the tears began to run down her cheeks.

"Ella?" said Nathan.

"Oh, dear," said Sarah. "I'm afraid I scared her."

"Scared her? How?" said Nathan.

"By telling her about birthing. That on top of the emotions she's going through, I better go to her."

"No. I'll go." He put his napkin on the table and followed Ella to their bedroom. Opening the door, he saw her sitting on the bed, her head down. Knocking lightly on the door, he alerted her to his presence.

She lifted her head, sniffled and quickly ducked her head again. "I'm sorry Nathan. I…I had to leave. I don't know what's the matter with me."

He strode to the bed sat down and wrapped her in his arms. "It's okay. You're just pregnant. Sarah says you're extra emotional now. John told me Sarah cried at the drop of a hat when she was carrying Sam."

Ella nodded her head then buried her face in his chest and bawled. He just held her and let her get it out. What else could he do? She didn't know why she was crying and he sure couldn't help if she couldn't tell him what was wrong.

She finally stopped, took the hanky from her cuff and blew her nose. Her eyes were red and puffy. He didn't think she'd want to go back to the dinner table, but he offered to escort her.

"Are you ready to get something to eat? You didn't eat much before you left."

"No. I can't go back yet." She got up and went to the cheval mirror standing in the corner. "Just look at me. I look awful. I'm not hungry anyway. I'd rather stay here and rest for a bit. I'll come back in a little while. Alright?"

"Sure. I'll explain to John and Sarah, but I know they already understand. Probably better than we do since they've been through it."

She nodded.

"Sarah told me she might have scared you with her talk of birthing. Surely it's not that bad. Arapaho women do it all the time with little fuss."

"I doubt you really know what they go through, but even if you're right, I'm not Arapaho. I'm like Sarah. She tells me that I won't even think about the pain afterwards, but I'm scared, Nathan.

What if something goes wrong?"

He patted the bed beside him. She sat next to him, her hands clenched in her lap. She'd never rest if she didn't relax.

"We'll have the doctor here and Sarah and Martha. I'll even be with you if it will make you feel better. Ella," he took her cold hand in his, the warmth spreading through her just from his touch. "We'll get through this together. You aren't alone."

She laid her head on his shoulder. Releasing her hands he hugged her to him.

"Thank you. I needed to hear that. It helps. Sometimes I feel so alone."

"You'll never be alone." The fierceness in his voice surprised her. "As long as I live you will never be alone. You're my wife and soon we'll have a beautiful son or daughter and you'll be wishing you had time alone."

Ella laughed. "You're probably right. I don't have two daughters to keep him occupied when I need time to myself, like Sarah does. You should get back to dinner before they get worried.

I'll be there soon."

He gave her a tender kiss. "Put a cool cloth on your eyes and lay down for a few minutes. It'll help relax you."

"I will. Now go."

Ella watch him leave and took his advice, pouring the tepid water from the pitcher into the basin on the commode. She put the wash cloth in and then wrung it out and folded it in thirds. She laid the folded cloth on her eyes after she laid down on the bed. The cloth cooled as the air hit it and felt wonderful on her swollen eyes. She was so tired. It was so nice to just relax for a little while.

When she woke the room was dark. Dinner! She'd slept through it and it would appear supper as well. She lit the kerosene lamp on the beside table. The clock on the dresser said nine o'clock. John and Sarah would be long gone by now and everyone else would be to bed if not asleep. Where was Nathan?

Her stomach grumbled. She'd missed two meals and was absolutely famished. She left the bedroom and headed for the kitchen. As she passed Nathan's office she saw the light beneath the door. She knocked.

"Come in."

"Good evening." She closed the door behind her. "Why didn't you wake me?"

"You needed the sleep. It was a stressful day and I want you healthy and that means rested."

She walked over to him, leaned down and gave him a kiss on the cheek.

He grasped her by the waist and pulled her down onto his lap. "I think you can do better than that."

"Oh!" She cradled his handsome face in her hands, his whiskers rough against her palms and captured his lips with hers. Her stomach growled.

Nathan pulled back chuckling. "I guess we better feed you first."

"That's where I was headed before I got waylaid."

"I'll go with you. I could use a snack."

"Come on then, I'll fix us both something to

eat."

They walked in companionable silence. When they reached the kitchen Nathan lit the lamps while Ella checked the ice box for leftovers.

"Looks like there's some cobbler left and we have some cream to go over it. Want me to heat it up?"

"No, cold sounds good to me. You should probably have something more substantial since you missed most of your meals today."

"I'm fine. This will hold me until breakfast. I'll make sure to eat better then."

"Are you sure? You're eating for two now."

She laughed. "I'm eating for one and a tiny little person who doesn't eat much yet."

The cobbler hit the spot. Her stomach was satisfied and the sweet treat left her sleepy.

"I'm ready to go back to bed. You wouldn't think I'd still be tired after sleeping all afternoon and part of the night, but I am."

"Oh, I bet I can get you a little energized."

She looked over at Nathan and melted

seeing the passion in his eyes. Would it always be such for her? All he had to do was look at her and she was putty in his hands. Wanting him and willing to do anything to get him. How long until he tired of her? Soon she'd be big as a house, then what? How would he still find her desirable?

Nathan came and stopped next to her chair then squatted down beside her. "What is going through that pretty little head of your? You have such a serious expression on your face."

"What are you going to do when I'm big as the barn? How can you want me then?"

"Ella, I will always want you. You're my wife and that is a bond I will never have with anyone else. It is a sacred bond with me. Is it with you? Will you desire someone else when you get tired of me?"

She shook her head. "Never. I could never love anyone else." She clapped her hand over her mouth realizing too late what she'd let out.

"Ella, I..."

Moving her hand from her mouth she placed

two fingers over Nathan's lips. "Shh. I know. Don't say anything. I shouldn't have said what I did."

Nathan rose and took Ella in his arms. "If I could love you, I would. You make it very easy." His lips crashed down on hers.

She returned his kiss with more passion than she'd ever felt. Fisting her hands in his hair she pressed her lips to his and waged war with his tongue. Both of them were breathless when they broke apart.

Nathan swept her up in his arms.

"Take me to bed. Show me that you desire me. Please, Nathan."

"My pleasure."

She held the lamp while he carried her quickly to their bedroom. He set her down in the center of the room. She put the lamp on the bedside table and turned back to him. Unbuttoning the buttons on her dress slowly, she teased her husband.

He'd sat down on the bed to take off his boots and now lay back on his elbows and watched the striptease she did for him, seemingly enjoying the show if his erection was any indication. Her dress dropped in a pile at her feet. Next she pulled the string on her chemise taking just an inch at a time, on and on until she had it opened to the waist. Once she reached her bloomers, she pulled their string firmly untying it and letting them fall to join her dress on the floor.

Her chemise covered her to the middle of her thighs. Still hiding all her treasures from Nathan's view. She sashayed over to the bed.

"Would you stand, please?"

He got up. He was breathing heavily and strained against the buttons of his pants.

She began unbuttoning his shirt. Too slow to suit his tastes, he ripped it over his head, shucking it along with his pants and drawers in record speed, the likes of which she hadn't seen since their wedding night.

"It looks like you're happy to see me." She smiled coyly or at least what she thought was coyly.

"You have no idea." He ripped open her

chemise baring her to his hungry gaze.

"You've put on weight with the baby…in all the right places." He bent his neck and took one turgid nipple into his mouth.

"Oh, God, Nathan. I love it when you do that."

He let it pop out. "I know," he said with a chuckle. "And you hate it when I stop."

"Yes, unless it's to kiss me elsewhere. Now stop talking and put that mouth of yours to good use."

"Yes, ma'am. Never let it be said that I left my wife unsatisfied."

He worked his way down her body until her knees started to shake. He backed her up and then followed her to the bed, coming down upon her bracing himself on his forearms. He positioned his member at her entrance and work his way in, sliding up her tight passage, filling her, her body and her heart. He made slow, sweet love to her. Sara and Martha were right. He loved her. No one could make love so completely, so honestly without love.

She believed that. Unwilling to stay in a marriage without love, she had to believe it.

CHAPTER 7

"Hurry up, Martha. We have to get back here in time to finish supper."

"I'm coming." Martha appeared in the foyer tying her bonnet under her chin. "You know if you'd learn to drive the team one of us, namely me, could stay here and get some work done. And we wouldn't always be in such an all fired hurry."

Ella shook her head, shivers snaking their way down her spine. "I can't Martha. You know that. I tried."

Martha put her hand on Ella's shoulder, "Honey, you can't let one bad incident keep you from doing what needs doing. Keep you from

162

living your life, with all its dangers and all its rewards."

"You're lucky I get into the wagon. It's hard. First, I see the carriage accident, then the runaway buggy. I'm not even sure I should be riding in a wagon much less driving one, especially alone."

"You will. When the time is right you'll do it."

"I hope you're right, but that time is not today."

They walked out through the courtyard to where the buckboard waited. Nathan always had one of the men harness the team to the wagon and bring it up to the front of the house for her. They climbed up and took off for town.

*****

Martha pulled the buckboard to a stop in front of the mercantile.

"You fill our order here and then go to the feed store for the grain. Nathan wants six fifty pound bags this time because of the new cows."

Martha nodded and started up the steps in front of the store. She turned back when she reached the boardwalk. "And what will you be doing while I'm filling our orders?"

Ella lifted her chin just a bit in a small show of defiance. "I'm going to go invite Mr. Daniel Adams to dinner."

Martha raised her eyebrows." Whatever for? Does Nathan know?"

"I believe he's a cousin or something of mine. He resembles my father so much and I need to know. It would be wonderful to find out that there is more than just Joshua and I."

"If he looks so much like your daddy maybe he's yer brother. That'd mean yer daddy was not faithful to yer mama. Are ya sure ya wanna know?"

"Of course, I've thought of it. He appears to be older than both me and Joshua. So before he married Mother, Father could have had other relationships. Still if it's true, why keep him hidden?"

"Don't be naïve, girl. He'd be a bastard and

yer father wouldn't have wanted him around his legitimate children. He also wouldn't a wanted to rub yer mama's face in it, so to speak."

"I suppose. But I'm going to find out one way or another." She pulled out her handkerchief from her reticule and wiped her sweaty hands with it. I'll see you at the feed store. If I'm not there, I'll be at the Astor House. He's supposed to be staying there, according to Mr. Jones, the clerk in the mercantile."

Martha nodded and went into the store, while Ella made her way down Main Street then up the hill to the Astor House hotel.

Upon entering the lobby she spied Mr. Adams at the front desk.

She rushed over to him, calling as she went. "Mr. Adams. Oh, Mr. Adams. Are you checking out? I'm so glad I caught you."

"Mrs. Ravenclaw," he said in surprise. "Yes, I am heading back to New York."

"I wonder if you could give me a few minutes of your time. Perhaps even join us at the ranch for the night and catch the train tomorrow. I've so many questions."

"I'm afraid I don't understand. What is it you need from me, Mrs. Ravenclaw."

"First, please call me Ella."

"Very well, Ella. What would you have of me?"

"Well," she glanced down at the reticule she had in a death grip in her lap. "I believe that you and I are related. You," she looked up at him and rushed on. "You resemble my father greatly. Even more than my brother, Joshua."

"Who was your father?"

"His name was Robert Davenport."

"Davenport," they said at the same time.

"Yes," gasped Ella.

"I carry my mother's name. My father was Robert Davenport."

"You said 'was', so you know he was killed."

"Yes. Let's sit down where we can talk more privately."

He ushered her across the plush carpet in the lobby to two overstuffed chairs situated in front of the large, glass window.

"I heard," Daniel began, "Father was killed in a carriage accident and that his daughter barely survived. That was more than a year ago. You must be the daughter."

"I am. Can't you tell by the scars on my face?"

"I admit I noticed your scars. I would be less than truthful had I said otherwise. The fact that you survived is amazing. Your scars are badges of courage."

"That's what my husband says."

"Smart man."

Ella thought of Nathan and a small smile played across her face. "Yes, he is."

They spoke for a little longer and Ella knew she needed more than a couple of minutes to talk. They had so much to discuss.

"Mr. Adams…."

"Daniel."

"Yes, Daniel. There is so much I want to ask you and that we should talk about. Would you consider delaying your trip for a day or two and come with me back to the ranch? You can stay in our guest room so you wouldn't be putting out any more money to stay and I'm a pretty good cook, if I do say so myself."

"Well, I...,"

"Please say yes. I would love for Nathan to meet you again and for us to get to know each other. We have a lot of time to make up for."

He stayed silent, she assumed he mulled things over in his mind while Ella sat on pins and needles. Finally, he said, "Yes. Of course, what is one or two more days? I have some business to conclude here and then I can come out. Perhaps you can give me directions so I don't delay your getting home. We wouldn't want your husband to worry."

"How thoughtful of you. Of course, I can give you directions. Do you want me to write them down for you?"

"Yes, please. My memory isn't what it used to be."

Ella got up and went to the desk and asked the clerk for paper and pen and commenced to putting the directions down on the page. When she was done she carefully blew on it and then folded it over. She went back to where Daniel was still sitting and handed him the sheet.

"We eat dinner at one and supper at six. There is always plenty to eat, but if you're delayed I can fix you something when you get there."

He nodded. "Thank you. I'm not sure if I can conclude my business in time for dinner, but I should be there by supper. Don't worry about feeding me. I'll eat luncheon, I mean dinner, before I come out."

Ella laughed. "It takes some getting used to, dinner for luncheon and supper for dinner, but that's the way it's done in the west. There's a lot of things that aren't like New York."

"I've discovered that. Lack of indoor plumbing is something I don't think I'll ever get used to. I'm lucky this place has facilities inside."

"I better warn you then. We don't have a bathroom in the house. It's something I'm going to have done, but I haven't gotten around to talking to the plumber yet."

"Thank you for the warning," he said and they laughed.

She had another brother. Ella hadn't been this thrilled in a while.

*****

Daniel left the Astor House and headed directly for the Chicago Saloon. There he met Frank and Billy Joe Baker. He'd previously hired the Baker boys to kidnap Ella, now he informed them of his change of plans.

They sat in the back of the saloon at one of the tables. All the tables were round and at many of them poker games were going on. No one paid attention to the three men talking quietly at the back of the room. Piano music played, girls plied their wiles and got unsuspecting cowboys to buy them drinks of watered down whiskey.

"I don't want you to come into contact with Mrs. Ravenclaw at all. I am going to be staying at their ranch for a few days. What I want you to do is a little sabotage for me. Let's see if we can get rid of her and her husband. Find a place where you can watch the going's on of the ranch and then meet me tomorrow night in the hills behind the ranch. According to Ella's directions, the house sets right next to the foothills. That should give you plenty of places to watch from without being seen."

"Sure thing, boss. You wanna know afore we do it what we gonna do?"

"No. I'm going to help you. I want to help Ella and Nathan meet their maker."

The Baker boys laughed.

Daniel steepled his fingers, elbows on the table and smiled.

*****

Ella left the Astor House and found Martha still at the feed store. They had just finished loading the 300 pounds of grain on to the buckboard.

"Martha. Martha," she said, breathless, as she ran up the steps to the door where Martha stood watching the men load the buckboard. "You'll never guess. Mr. Adams is my brother."

"Your brother! It figures. Didn't I tell ya," scoffed Martha.

"It's true. He looks so much like father, I knew he had to be some relation to me. I thought it would be a cousin or something, but apparently not. Anyway to make a long story short, I invited him to the ranch for a few days." Ella stopped to breathe. "I'll prepare the guest room when we get home."

Martha frowned. "Don't you think you should've talked to Nathan first?"

Ella shook her head, no, and then preceded to adjust her gloves. "There wasn't time. He had his tickets and was checking out of the Astor House to return to New York."

"I don't know, Ella, it seems…."

Ella raised her hand, stopping Martha's words. "It's fate. We were meant to meet. That's all there is to it. Nathan will understand."

Nathan did not understand. "*You did what? This man says he's your long lost brother and you don't find that the least bit suspicious?*"

"Well I...."

He raged on. "Why didn't he come to you in New York. He's had more than a year since your father died to step forth and make his existence known to you and your brother."

"Nathan...."

"And what do you do? You simply accept it all like it's nothing unusual. Just a typical day."

She heaved a sigh. "You're right, I acted impulsively, but Nathan, if he went back to New York, I might never have had the opportunity to get to know him."

"Oh, I have a feeling you would have. I think he followed you here."

"How could he? He couldn't have known I was coming to this God-forsaken place." Her anger rose at each of Nathan's points. But was she angry with him or herself?

Nathan rolled his eyes. "Ella, he could have

been watching you for months. Waiting to see if you survived the accident. You know nothing about him. Will you just listen to yourself?"

"Mistake or not, he's coming here for a few days and I expect you to be civil. We are done here."

Nathan watched her walk from the room her back straight and stiff as a board. He slammed his fist against the wall, wishing it was Daniel Adams' face.

*****

Ella kept her back ramrod straight until she reached their bedroom. There she collapsed on the bed and let the tears flow down her face. All the things Nathan said were true. She'd invited a complete stranger into their home. And if Nathan was right, may have put them in danger.

No. She refused to believe that. Daniel looked too much like her father. She may have hurried things along, but she knew Daniel Adams was her brother. He was family. He would never hurt her.

*****

Nathan was sure this Daniel character followed Ella from New York. He may well be her long lost illegitimate brother, but why wait so long to show himself after her father's death? What was his game? It didn't feel right. He'd only met the man once, but even then it felt off. He reminded Nathan of the snake oil salesmen that occasionally came to town. Had Daniel been lying in wait for Ella? How long had he been in town?

Nathan had his own questions for Mr. Daniel Adams.

*****

Daniel arrived in a buggy from town. He probably didn't know how to ride a horse so had to bring the buggy. Nathan had one of his men unhitch the horse take it to the barn and put him in an empty stall after rubbing him down and giving him some oats.

Supper was just beginning when Daniel arrived. Ella had a chair brought in and sat him between herself and Nathan. Smart girl thought

Nathan. She was making sure he could hear the conversation as well. No doubt that Ella would keep him talking, plying him with questions about their father.

She didn't disappoint. Martha told her to stay with her guest. She, Martha, would clean up the kitchen. Ella moved herself, Nathan and Daniel to the parlor where it was more conducive to conversation and much more comfortable as well.

"Daniel, tell me about father. He would disappear for weekends and sometimes a week, saying he had business in Boston. Mother never questioned it. I only did after he was dead and Joshua never had to take those same trips. Now I assume he was visiting you and your mother."

He sipped his tea, which Ella fixed him especially, before answering. "Yes, we would see Father once a month for a weekend and then every few months for a week. My mother was always excited and she could barely contain herself the day before he came. It was the same each time. In their case, absence really did make the heart grow fonder."

Ella set down her tea cup. She didn't usually drink tea anymore. She said she preferred coffee, that it kept her going for all the work that needed doing each day. Apparently, that was only with Nathan. Just as well. He didn't like tea anyway.

The two of them talked until late. Nathan didn't add anything to the conversation and would have excused himself if it had been anyone other than Adams with Ella. For some reason he didn't feel safe leaving her alone with him.

Finally he'd had enough. "Adams, you must excuse us. I'm afraid we don't keep New York hours here. Work starts at daybreak on a ranch and earlier for Ella. We'll show you to your room."

Nathan held his hand out to Ella.

She looked up at him and took his hand without question. It pleased him immensely. "Yes, if you'll follow us, please. I've already had your bag taken to the room."

Nathan placed his hand on Ella's waist as

they walked side by side down the wide hall with Daniel following behind. Windows lined the courtyard side of the hall, light from the lamp Nathan carried bounced out into the dark night.

"You have quite an impressive home, Ravenclaw. It's unlike anything I've seen before."

"Thank you. I designed it myself based on some Mexican hacienda's I'd seen. I had them build it after the barn was built."

"Why would you build the barn first?"

"Because the animals are more important. Without them, there is no ranch and no need for a home."

"I see."

"Here we are." Nathan opened the door to the guest room, two doors down from theirs, went inside to the table by the bed and lit the lamp there. It was a small room, compared to theirs, but had all the necessary amenities needed for a guest...bed, wardrobe, commode and chamber pot. "See you in the morning for breakfast. Ella bangs the triangle to call the men to breakfast. Of course, if you're up you can come down to the kitchen before that. There's always coffee on the stove."

"Yes, good night," said Ella.

Daniel took her hand and kissed it. "Good night, sweet sister. See you in the morning." He went into the room and closed the door behind him.

Nathan pressed Ella forward to their room. As soon as the door was closed behind them, he gathered her into his arms. "I thought the evening was never going to end," he said just before his lips found hers. He wanted to brand her and seared her with his kiss. His beautiful Ella, responded as she always did. He loved her passion.

She wrapped her arms around his neck and pressed her body flush with his. Her tongue plunged into his mouth and danced with his. It always surprised him when she did this, but pleased him that she wanted to take the lead. She gave as much as she took. Breathless, he broke away, placed his hand on her stomach and said, "Mine. You are both *mine*."

She smiled, her hand atop his, "Yours.

Ours."

He swung her up into his arms and carried her to bed. By the time he was done there would be no question who she belonged to.

CHAPTER 8

Daniel waited for two hours after they'd dropped him at his room before he ventured forth. Taking the lamp from his bedside he made his way to the hillside. The Baker brothers met him there.

"Boss, the barn is behind the house. It'll be where you'll find the buggy."

"Good. Let's go."

Daniel followed the Bakers to the barn where they found what looked to be the most worn saddle and Frank cut partially through the main strap, up high, under the saddle where it was less likely to be seen. Hopefully, if he was lucky, Nathan would be the one using it and it wouldn't give out until after Daniel left.

While Frank did the saddle, Bobby Joe sawed the axle on the buggy, just where Daniel showed him. It wouldn't take too much for it to break clean through. Just a couple of good jolts. If they were going fast enough, it should throw whoever from the buggy, or better yet, drag them when the horses don't stop.

He let the Bakers do the actual sabotage. Daniel refused to get his hands dirty with the labor involved, just wanted to make sure it got done right and quickly. He had no intention of going back to New York until he was sure Ella and Nathan were both eliminated. That would leave Joshua still alive and hopefully Daniels' associates would resolve that issue before his return. He felt sure Ella was all that remained between him and his rightful inheritance.

*****

Daniel spent two nights with them. The second night was not any more comfortable for Nathan than the first had been. All in all, having a tooth pulled was preferable to spending another evening listening to them ply each other with questions and then share what he was sure they thought were amusing stories. It did sound like Daniel really was Ella's brother. That didn't mean Nathan trusted him. Far from it. Daniel Adams was one of the least trustworthy men he'd ever met.

Thank goodness he was gone. Supposedly, back to New York. Out of their lives forever if Nathan had his way, though he didn't relax his guard on Ella. He didn't really believe Daniel went back East but he had a mustang round up to do, though he wasn't about to leave Ella unprotected. There was one man left at the ranch with explicit instructions to watch over Ella. Nathan would be gone for a week and he already missed her soft touch. He was starting to get used to a lot about Ella. Whenever he was away overnight, he missed her sweet rose scent, her lively conversation and the welcoming comfort of her body.

Just the thought of them in bed made him hard. The memory of his rough hand on her nipples…. He had to stop thinking about it. The more he did the more painful the ride became.

"Herd up ahead," one of the cowboys called back.

"Alright, you all know what to do. Surround them and drive them to the corral."

They'd roped off a makeshift corral in a copse of pine trees. It was large enough for about ten horses. This stallion and his harem were eight horses. The stallion, four mares and three foals. Just the foals alone would make this trip worth while. They could be raised to be incredible mounts.

Nathan kicked his horse into a gallop after the herd. In and out of the trees, around them, right and left. The stallion led them on a merry chase through the trees. Nathan gained on him, his own mustang the fastest he had and one of the fastest horses he'd ever seen. He'd have no trouble running this stallion to ground. The stallion cut sharp right, Nathan followed. He felt the saddle give as he went one way and his horse another.

He saw the rock just before he felt it. Then he saw nothing.

Pain. Shooting through his arm and behind his eyes.

"Boss. You okay? Nathan?"

He heard rather than saw his foreman, the pain in his head too intense to open his eyes.

"Jeb? What? What happened?"

"The strap on yer saddle broke. Ya fell off and hit yer head on a rock. Purty lucky it didn't kill ya."

"I don't feel lucky right now. What's wrong with my arm? It hurts like hell."

"Looks like it's busted. Probably when ya hit the ground. I got one of the boys looking for a couple straight sticks. We'll get it set afore we head back,"

Nathan tried to nod. "Ow. Shit. That hurts." He closed his eyes tight and put his right hand over them.

"Don't move yer head, boss. Yer bleedin'. Soon as we get ya back to camp, I'll have Cookie get ya cleaned up. Then we ken head on back home."

"Did we get the horses? Tell me we got that big appaloosa stallion."

"We did." He could hear the smile in Jeb's voice. "Got 'em all. They'll be comin' home with us."

Nathan forced his eyes open. Stars were exploding in his brain, but at least they were little stars now. "What in the hell happened? Did you get my horse and saddle?"

"Sure did. Like I said, looks like the strap on the saddle gave way."

"Impossible. Those straps were all replaced not two months ago. Check it again."

"Yes, sir," he said and left to get the saddle.

Nathan sat up, but his head spun and he had to lie back down. He tried more slowly, keeping his left arm at his waist and lifting himself with his right arm. He was a mess and, if he was right, damned lucky to be alive.

Jeb came running back to him. "You was

right. The strap was cut. Not clean through, but enough that it broke when stressed like you did riding after that stallion."

Nathan swallowed hard, his throat dry as the dirt he sat in. "Give me your canteen. Please."

Jeb got the canteen from his saddle and handed it to him. He took a long swig and was finally able to speak clearly. "Gather up the men and bring me my horse. As soon as you get this arm set, I'm riding back home. You and the men follow with the horses. Put my saddle in the chuck wagon. I want to take a good look at it when we get back home."

"Boss, you can't ride by yerself all that way bareback, you bein' busted up an all."

"Don't worry about it, Jeb, I'm used to it. That's how I learned to ride. I'm half Indian, remember?"

"Yes, sir. I forgot. Me and the men will be home in a few days."

One of the cowboys came up with two fairly straight tree branches. Jeb handed Nathan a small stick to bite down on while he straightened his arm. They didn't want him to bite his tongue by accident when the pain got to him. Once it was in his mouth, Nathan nodded and Jeb pulled the arm until the bones were in line again. Then he placed a branch on either side of the arm, tying them tight with strips of cloth torn from the bottom of Nathan's shirt. It was already ripped across the shoulder, no reason not to use it to bind his arm.

With his left arm broken, he needed a leg up on his stallion, but once there he kicked him into a gallop toward home. To Ella. His Ella. She had to be safe. What if Daniel was there right now? What if he'd hurt her? Nathan rode as hard and fast as he could. The terrain kept him from running the horse too long. It was hilly and rocky followed by long valleys where he could let the horse have its head. It was the longest four hours of his life.

He jumped off the horse on the side of the house by the kitchen door knowing Ella was most likely there. Slamming open the door his heart sank when he didn't see her or Martha. He ran from room to room, calling for Ella, but they weren't in the house. What if they went to town? Daniel was probably still there. Nathan had no doubt that he didn't return to New York, he'd want to see the results of his handiwork. Nathan didn't know or care about the reason behind it, he only knew Ella was in danger.

He ran to the barn. The buggy was gone. They could have gone to town or to John and Sarah's, whose place was on the way to town. He started out of the barn, then stopped and, acting on a hunch, went over to where the buggy had been parked and found what he was looking for. It sent chills racing down his spine. Sawdust.

Running as fast as his long legs would carry him toward the house, he ran into Seth, the cowboy he'd left with Ella.

"Where is she?"

"Whoa, boss, what happened to yer arm?"

"Nevermind me." Nathan grabbed him by the front of his shirt with his right hand nearly lifting the cowboy off the ground. "Where is she?

Where is Ella?"

Seth's eyes got wide. "She..she and Martha were going to the J bar A."

"How long have they been gone?" he released his grip on Seth.

"Not long. Half hour maybe."

"Why didn't you go with her?"

"They was only going a little way and Martha was with her. Missus Ella said they'd be alright and I agreed with her. So I stayed to do my chores."

Nathan's chest constricted. "Come with me. I need help onto my horse." He set off at a run for the house where Seth helped him on the horse. He didn't explain anything, just kicked the horse and galloped down the road. Toward Ella. Toward his heart.

*****

Ella walked into the kitchen where Martha was putting away the last of the dinner dishes.

"Get your coat. We're going to the Atwoods and maybe then on to town. I need some more material for baby clothes." She pressed her hand against her stomach. Clearly pregnant now at about five months, she wondered when she would feel the baby kick. The doctor said it would be any time now, said it took longer for first time mothers.

Martha put the last plate in the cupboard and said, "Let me get Seth so he can come with us."

"That's not necessary. You're with me. I think Nathan's being a little over protective."

"I don't know," she hedged.

"Come on, Martha. Seth's got chores that need to be done here. There's no need for him to be tagging along with us."

"Well, I guess it'll be alright. It's not far and we can always come home if you get tired."

"Tired!? It's a rest not to be doing housework and cooking for eighteen people every day. I hate to admit it, but this has been like a vacation since the men went after the mustangs."

Martha chuckled. "It has been, hasn't it? Don't tell Nathan. He's probably missing you somethin' fierce."

"I doubt that. Nathan doesn't love me. If I wasn't pregnant—"

"Now stop right there. I told ya before. Of course, Nathan loves you. Don't ya see the way he acts, touching ya all the time, guiding you from the room with his hand on yer waist. Kissing ya every time he comes in, no matter who's here. Sitting with ya every night after supper rather than go to his office like he used ta."

"He's just being polite and possessive of me because of the baby. He doesn't love me. He told me so."

Martha rolled her eyes. "He's scared. He don't wanna be hurt again." She put her hands on her hips and cocked her head to one side. "And I don't suppose you love him either. Ya just blush every time he looks at cha and you just sit there with yer heart in yer eyes every time he's in the room."

Ella sucked in a breath. "I don't."

Martha grinned. "Ya do. You two are the most stubborn and, obviously blind people I know.

Everyone else sees it."

Ella could believe her ears. Martha and Sarah had both told her that Nathan loved her but he insisted he didn't believe in love. How could he love her if he didn't believe it possible? Her heart quickened and for some reason just thinking about him made her a little breathless.

"Does it really show that much?"

"Almost since the day you got here."

"Oh, Martha. What am I going to do? What if you're wrong? What if he can't let himself love me?"

"First we're going to get in the buggy and get to the Atwoods. Then you have to convince him to let go. Let go of the past, of the hurt, of the fear and to live for the future with you and that little one growin' in yer belly."

"I don't know how."

They walked out to the front of the house. Seth had brought the buggy around and was holding the team in place waiting for Ella and Martha. He helped Ella in, while Martha hopped up on the other side.

Martha picked up the reins. "Thank ya Seth. We'll be back soon." She slapped the reins on the horses, not waiting for an answer from Seth.

After a few minutes, she said, "Talk to him, Ella. Yer both smart and you'll figure it out."

Ella teared up. She seemed to do that a lot more lately. She knew it was the changes because of the baby, Sarah had told her about them, but that didn't make her like it any better. "I can't. I can't risk the possible rejection."

"Well, knowing Nathan, yer gonna have to make the first move."

She took a deep breath and the tears abated. "I could make a special supper for just the two of us and serve it in our room."

Martha nodded and then grinned. "That's a good start. But with you two, you might never get to supper. Maybe Sarah has some better ideas." She slapped the butts of the horses. "Giddy up."

They turned onto the road leading to the Atwoods house. Just a couple of minutes and they'd be there and then she could grill Sarah. John and Sarah obviously loved each other, but it couldn't have always been that way. Sarah was a mail order bride just like Ella, yet somehow they'd fallen in love.

Just as they pulled up in front of the house, the buggy gave a loud creak and dropped to the ground. As it hit, Ella and Martha were thrown from the vehicle.

"Ella! Martha! John! Come quick." Sarah shouted as she ran down the porch stairs to the buggy.

"I'm fine," said Martha. She got up off the ground and dusted herself off. "How's Ella?"

"I think I'm okay." She had landed on her hands and knees. She rolled over, sat in the dirt and took off her gloves. There were abrasions on her palms, but no blood. Her leather gloves had protected her hands. The same couldn't be said for her knees. Her dress was torn and her knees both had cuts from the rocks.

Sarah stopped by Ella and looked at her

knees. "They're not bad. Can you get up? Here let me help you? How is the baby?" She extended her hand to Ella and pulled her to her feet.

"The baby is fine. What in the world just happened?"

John had come running when Sarah yelled. He looked at the buggy. "The axle broke. If this had happened while you were moving along the road, you both could have been killed."

Ella's breath caught. She remembered the carriage accident in New York. But that couldn't have happened here. MacGregor couldn't be here. Unless it wasn't MacGregor that tried to kill her in New York. She couldn't think about that right now.

She turned at the sound of the pounding of horses hooves. There was Nathan bearing down on them at a full gallop.

"Ella!" he called, sliding to a stop in back of the broken carriage. "Ella, are you all right?" He ran to her and wrapped her in his embrace. "Are you hurt?"

"No. But you are," she pulled back from

him. "Oh, my God, what happened to you?"

"It's nothing." He hugged her again as much as he could with one good arm and one braced with tree branches. "I've never been so scared in my life."

"When you broke your arm?" She hugged him back, very glad and very surprised to see him.

"No. When I saw the sawdust."

"Sawdust?"

Nathan looked over at John who was examining the axle. "Tell me I'm wrong. Tell me the axle wasn't cut."

John shook his head. "Can't do it. It was definitely cut, but not all the way through. It was meant to break while traveling. Whoever did this was trying to kill someone."

All the women sucked in a breath, stunned at what John said.

"Damn," said Nathan, "I'd hoped for Ella's sake I was wrong."

Sarah spoke up. "Everyone come inside. I need to get Ella cleaned up and we need to do some talking, by the sounds of it."

They walked inside. Nathan put his good arm around Ella's shoulders and she put her arm around his waist. Neither of them wanted to let the other go. For Ella, she needed reassurance that he was okay.

They all went to the kitchen. Bertha was already there. When she saw everyone come in and the state of Ella's dress she said, "I'll put on a fresh pot of coffee. I have a feeling it's going to be a long afternoon."

Sarah got a basin of warm water, some wash cloths and a towel. She cleaned Ella's knees and hands with lye soap. It stung even though Ella was sure she was trying to be gentle, but when Sarah brought out the iodine, Ella stopped her.

"You are not putting that stuff on me. It stings like hell," she said cursing like she'd heard Nathan do. "We've got some salve we'll put on at home."

"Horse liniment," said Nathan absently.

"Horse liniment! You put horse liniment on

me?"

"It worked didn't it? And it didn't hurt did it?"

"Well, yes it worked and no, it didn't hurt, but the thought—"

"Then don't complain unless you want the iodine."

She hushed, but was not happy.

They sat around a huge, rectangular oak table, big enough to seat twenty people. John and his family ate with his employees, just as she and Nathan did. They rarely used the dining room unless they had guests. Even then it was only because the kitchen table simply couldn't hold any more people.

"Nathan, you start. What happened to you? You're a mess," said John.

"The strap on my saddle tore. I went one way and my horse went another."

"Oh, Nathan, I'm so sorry," said Ella.

"Honey, it's not your fault." He squeezed her hand and smiled at her.

That just made it worse. "But it is." She started to cry, unable to keep the tears at bay.

"Ella, honey, calm down." Nathan sat next to her and put his arm around her shoulders. "It's okay, I'm fine."

She pushed away from him enough to look up at his face. His beloved face, now covered with scratches and bruises and a cut on his forehead. "You're not fine. Your arm is broken and you've a wound on your forehead, which needs cleaning. Now."

"Not now. It's fine."

"Yes. Now. I need to do it now. I'll explain everything while I do it."

Sarah brought her some fresh water and towels.

Ella took the bandage off and gasped. "Nathan. This is terrible. How were you able to ride?"

"I had more important things to worry about. You and this baby." He rubbed his hand slowly across her belly, but looked up at her.

200

She smiled at his possessiveness of the baby.

Ella started talking as she cleaned his head wound. "You all know I was in a carriage accident. It's what left me with these scars. It wasn't an accident. The axle broke just like the one today, in almost the exact same place. Except we were moving at a good clip, Father was late for a meeting. The horses dragged the carriage, tearing it apart and us with it. Father was killed. After our investigator's findings, Joshua and I knew someone was trying to kills us."

She stopped, her mouth dry. After wrapping a new bandage around Nathan's head, she picked up her cup and took a large swallow of her now cold coffee.

"We thought it was Father's former business partner, Angus MacGregor. Thought he wanted us out so he could get back into the business, but now I'm sure it wasn't him. He's not here. He couldn't have cut the axle and someone else wouldn't have known to cut it in the exact same place. But…"

"Daniel could." Nathan finished for her.

She nodded and broke into tears again.

Nathan took her hand and pulled her onto his lap.

"I brought him to the ranch, into our home. He would have had plenty of opportunity to saw through the axle."

"And cut the strap on my saddle."

Ella gasped.

"But none of that is your fault. You had no way of knowing."

"You never said the strap was cut," said John.

"Coffee's done," interrupted Bertha. "Who wants some?"

"Serve everyone, Bertha. We're all going to need it," said Sarah.

"Don't you see? It's all my fault. I let him—"

"No, you didn't," said Nathan. "Daniel followed you here. Don't you see? He waited until he *happened* to run into you. Then he stayed just long enough for his resemblance to your father to trigger your memories. He knew you'd come find him."

"You knew something was wrong. I just didn't want to see it. I miss Joshua so much, I thought finding Daniel was a God send," she wept.

Nathan didn't say anything. He just wrapped her in his arms as best he could and let her cry. It was the sweetest thing he could have done. Finally, she got a hold of herself and stopped crying. Now she was just mad.

"You don't believe that he went back to New York do you?" she asked Nathan.

"No. I think he'll want to make sure his handiwork was successful. I'm sure he didn't stay at the Astor House either, but if he's not in Golden then he's in Denver. He's too much a city boy to be camping anywhere near."

"Can't we can get the sheriff to search the area hotels?" asked Sarah.

"In Golden it would work, there are still few enough of them, but if he went to ground in Denver, like William did, we won't find him," said John.

Ella watched a shudder pass through Sarah and she moved close to John. "Who's William?"

"William was Sarah's cousin. He was obsessed with her and when he couldn't have her he decided to kill her."

"He threatened MaryAnn, too," added Sarah. "John had to kill him."

"I wish I could kill Daniel," muttered Nathan.

"I can understand that," said Ella. "I never thought I'd feel that way about anyone, but I wish I could kill him, too. He killed Father and now he's tried to kill you. If he's not stopped he'll eliminate everyone I love."

Nathan's arm tightened around her waist. "I take it that you love me then." He said it so softly she would have missed it if he hadn't said it directly into her ear.

"I…I," she dropped her head to her chest. "I didn't want you to know it," she whispered back.

He kissed her cheek. "You can't take it back now."

She shook her head.

"I don't know what you two are doing, but we need to figure out what to do about Daniel," said John with a smile.

Ella looked up when he spoke and then felt herself blush at the knowing smile on John's face.

"There's not much we can do until he makes another attempt. I have a feeling his next try won't be something so subtle," said Nathan. "I'm going to go about business as usual. Let him know it didn't work and try to force his hand."

"Do you think that's wise?" asked Ella.

"We don't have much choice unless we want to live the rest of our lives looking over our shoulders, waiting for him to try again." He looked over at John. "I'd like to borrow your carriage to take my girls home. I'll have one of my men bring it back."

"Of course. Keep it as long as you need it."

Nathan nodded. "I want to get Ella home now. It's been a trying day for her."

"I'm fine."

"You might as well stay for supper. Ella doesn't want to cook after a day like today," said Sarah.

"On the contrary, I think fixing supper is exactly what I need to get my mind off of it. But first we need to get Nathan to a doctor so he can get these tree limbs off his arm. He looks a little ridiculous." She smiled at her poor husband.

They all laughed.

CHAPTER 9

Ella refused to sit inside the coach and rode on top, sitting to Nathan's right.

"So," he said slowly, "you said you love me."

She fiddled with her gloves. "I didn't."

"Not exactly, but it's true nonetheless."

"You can't be sure of that."

He chuckled. "Defiant to the end. Well, I realized something today. Hit me like a ton of rock when I was scared I'd be too late to save you."

"It was rock. The rock you hit your head on."

"No. This was something different."

"Oh and what's that?"

He turned to her, his eyes dark blue in the fading light. "I realized you are the most important thing to me. I love you, Ella. I thought I would die trying to get to you and knew I would if I lost you."

She ducked her head. "Because of the baby."

He rested the reins on her knee and then gave it a squeeze. "Look at me. I love you, Ella. *You.* I have for quite a long time, maybe since you gave yourself so sweetly to me the first time. The baby is icing on the cake, but you, you are my first love."

"Your first love? What about Hettie? Martha told me you loved her."

The carriage rocked gently as they traveled along the road. The motion would have been soothing if not for the butterflies flying around in her stomach.

"I thought I did, but what I felt for her was nothing compared to my love for you. I never loved her. Not really. I wanted her and thought I loved her, but I know now I didn't. It was just infatuation. Wanting something I couldn't have. It probably would have ended the first time I bedded her."

He tried to put the reins in his left hand, but it didn't work, so he kept them in his right. "Damn." He brought his left hand to her face. The fingers were swollen and she was sure it was painful for him to move it, but then he touched her. Feather light touches on her right cheek.

She stilled and closed her eyes. Then she leaned ever so gently into his fingers. "Oh, Nathan. I do love you, so much. I have since the second you treated my sores. You were so sweet. I couldn't believe that a big, strong man like you could be so gentle."

He kissed her. "I'm still angry about that infernal contraption."

She laughed. "I know. I had to hide them so you wouldn't burn them."

"At least there's no way you can wear it now," he grumbled.

"I wouldn't anyway. I've discovered I like

the freedom I have without it."

"Good."

It was nearly dark now. He handed her the reins. "Here, hold these a minute while I light the lamp." He took a match from his pants pocket and lit the lantern hanging on the pole to his left.

She handed him back the reins and placed her hand in his lap. He hardened under her finger tips. "Without the corset I have the freedom to get up here and ride with you. Or," she fell to her knees at his feet. The fit was tight, but she managed. "To be able to love you with my mouth, now, on our way home."

After undoing the buttons on his pants she released him into her waiting hand, caressed him and felt the small drop of moisture on the end of his rod.

He groaned.

Gratified, she smiled up at him and then ran her tongue over his throbbing member, all the while watching his face, gauging his reaction.

He stiffened, straightening his legs as much

as the cramped space allowed and rose to meet her descending mouth.

"God, Ella. More."

She quickly obliged, taking him as far as she could into her mouth. The space was too small for her to get a position that allowed her to take more than half of him.

Suddenly, he put his hand on her head. "As much as I would like to continue this, there's a light coming our way. We've got to stop now. But," he grinned at her and cocked one midnight brow, "I mean to continue when we get home."

She got up, fastened his pants for him then sat back and straightened her own clothes. By the time the oncoming wagon reached them you'd never know they'd been doing anything other than driving home.

Nathan pulled the team to the side of the road and stopped, waiting for the on comer to pass. When they got abreast of them, the man pulled his buckboard to a stop.

"Hello there, Nathan. Ella. What are you

doing out? Thought this was round up time." It was their neighbor to the north, Caleb Black.

"Hello, Caleb. Came home early. Had a bit of an accident." Nathan raised his arm with the tree branches still on it.

Caleb chuckled. "I can see that. Looks like you had a run in with a tree and the tree won. Got a broken arm I'd guess from those limbs attached to you."

"Yes, I do. Hey, are you headed to town?"

"Sure am."

"Could you stop by Doc Smith's and ask him to come out to the ranch? I need him to check Ella as well as see to this arm."

"Sure. I'll go first thing. He still might make it out tonight if he's at the office."

"Thanks, Caleb. Have a good night."

"You folks, too."

Nathan turned back to the horses and flicked the reins on their butts. "Giddy up."

Not long after that they turned down the drive to the ranch.

"I'm going to pay you back for tonight when we get home," he said, promise in his eyes.

"Not right away you won't. We have to wait up for the doctor, but when we go to bed I expect your undivided attention."

They pulled to a stop in front of the courtyard. "You'll have it. Now give your poor suffering husband a kiss."

She took his face between her palms, careful of his hurts and kissed him gently. He would have none of it. He dropped the reins and pulled her close, his tongue delving deep. Tasting her, feasting on her. She shivered in response, returning each thrust, dueling, playing.

Someone cleared their throat.

They broke apart.

Seth stood in front of the team, holding them still. "Um, I'll get these put away for you, boss."

Nathan jumped down and came around to help Ella down.

Martha clattered out of the back. "Nice ride there, Nathan. Got in a little nap 'til we met Caleb on the road. Nice of him to send the doc out." Martha winked at them.

Ella was mortified. Her gaze flew to Nathan. He grinned then barked with laughter.

*****

The doctor arrived a couple of hours after they got home.

"Doctor Smith," said Ella as she led the short, balding man back to the kitchen where Nathan waited. "It's so good of you to come out and see us tonight. I'm sure Nathan is feeling the pain from his injuries now that the excitement has worn off."

"Yes, well Caleb said Nathan looked a mess and that I was to check you over, too. What happened?" The doctor set his bag on the table and opened it. He had a second bag with him that he set beside the first. From the first bag he took out a stethoscope. He listened to Ella's heart and lungs then listened for the baby's heartbeat.

"Everything sounds good. Baby's heartbeat is good and strong. Now tell me what happened here."

"We had a couple of accidents today," said Nathan. "I want you to check Martha, too. She was in the buggy with Ella when the axle broke."

"I'm fine," said Martha. "My hands are a little scraped that's all. Nothing compared to Ella and he said she's fine."

"Scrapes? Let me see, young lady," he said to Ella. "And you," he pointed to Martha, "just wait right there, I'll get you next. From the look of it, you're both all right, but Nathan is going to take a while and he seems to be more concerned with you two than himself, so just sit right down."

Doc Smith checked both Ella and Martha. "Sarah did a good job cleaning these cuts on your knees. I think both you and Martha are fine. It's a lucky thing too. It sounds like it was a bad situation. I've seen accidents like that kill people. Now Nathan, let's get a look at you and get that arm in a cast. Martha get in that second bag there and take out all the linen strips, then put two quarts of warm water into a basin and put the contents of the sack in the water. Mix it up good so there's no lumps, then put the linen strips in to soak."

Martha took the paper bag full of a white powder and stirred it into the water.

"Ella, you might want to go wait for me in the bedroom," said Nathan. "Martha can help Doc if he needs it."

"No. I want to stay with you," she insisted.

"What I really need is another man. Are all your men gone?" asked Doc.

"No. Honey," Nathan said to Ella, "why don't you go see if Seth can come up here to help the doc."

Ella kissed him on the cheek and left to find Seth.

Doc worked quickly to get Nathan's arm unwrapped and Nathan out of his shirt while Ella was gone. Resetting the arm was not a pretty thing to watch, especially if you're pregnant and it's someone you love.

"Martha, I need one of Nathan's socks. Cut the toe off and about an inch and a half below the top cut out a hole big enough for his thumb to go through."

"This ain't my first rodeo, Doc. Be right back," she said as she left.

After Martha left Doc told Nathan, "This is probably going to hurt like hell. You got any whiskey around here?"

"There's a bottle in the pantry. Top shelf."

Doc got the whiskey and handed it to Nathan. "Take a couple big swigs."

Nathan took three gulps and felt the burn all the way down with each one.

"Now. Your arm is misaligned, whether from the tree limbs or waiting so long to come to me, I don't know. I'm going to have to align it properly. It's going to amount to re-breaking it. I want you to bite down on this piece of rawhide. I'm going to do it now before the women come back. Hold on."

Doc took his arm, pulled and pushed until the bones were in the right place. About that time Martha returned with the sock. He put it on

Nathan's arm then wrung out the first of the linen strips and wrapped it around the arm.

Ella came back with Seth in tow.

"Sorry, Seth. Looks like I won't need you after all."

"That's okay, Doc. Glad I was here in case ya did."

Doc continued wrapping until all the linen had been used and then took the last of the plaster and patted it on Nathan's wrist.

"It's going to take this about six hours to dry. Do you have anything to make a sling out of?"

"Sure. That shirt." He pointed at his mangled shirt lying in a heap on the floor. "It's already torn up."

"Fine. Wear the sling for the next six weeks then come see me. Now I know you won't wear it all the time, but do it as often as you can. If you notice swelling, your fingers turning blue, anything like that, you come to see me. We'll redo the cast and give it some more room. Take some laudanum in water as you need it, most especially at night before bed. *Don't use that arm.* Hear me?"

"How am I supposed to work?"

Ella got a fresh basin of water and set it on the table in front of the doctor with a washcloth and a towel.

Doc cleaned up in the water. Soon it was white with plaster, but the doc's hands were clean. "I suggest you hire another man if you need to or divide your work up between the men you have. Confine yourself to paperwork. If you're like most ranchers I know you've got plenty of it to keep you busy for a while."

"We'll make sure he takes it easy," said Ella. She stood behind Nathan, her hand resting on his shoulder.

"See that you do." Doc picked up his bags and left.

Ella sent everyone to bed then made some laudanum water for Nathan. "Here drink this."

He frowned. "It's going to make me sleepy. I won't be able to stay awake long enough for you to take advantage of me."

"Darlin' there will be plenty of time to take advantage of you." She laughed. "Plenty of time."

They walked to their bedroom. Once there, Nathan shut the door behind them and pulled Ella into his arms. It was easier to do with the cast on instead of the tree limbs, but it was still awkward.

She pulled back and looked at him. "You need to let that dry."

He kissed her jaw just in front of her ear and then down her neck. "You need to stop worrying so much and help me out of these clothes."

She shook her head, but was more than happy to oblige and not surprised to find him stiff and ready.

"What do you think you're going to do with that?" she asked as she unbuttoned her dress and let it fall to the floor. It was quickly followed by her chemise and bloomers until she stood there in nothing but her stockings.

"Damn you look good. I think I'm going to make love to my wife." He bent his head and took one of her nipples in his mouth.

Ella gasped with pleasure, heat moving from her nipples straight down to her core. It didn't take much since the pregnancy. It seemed she wanted sex all the time which was fine with Nathan.

"You have to keep your arm elevated," she protested, though half-heartedly. "And it needs to dry."

"I know and I will. You're going to ride me tonight, my love. You're going to be on top. You'll set the pace. Have the control."

Ella grinned. "I have control? Oh, this is going to be fun. Lay back and put your arm above your head."

He did as she bade.

She climbed on top of him, her sex over his, brushing his member. She took it in her hand and guided it into her while bracing herself on his chest with her other hand. She slid down him, the fullness exquisite. Then she lifted herself slowly, feeling every hard inch of him. Repeating the movements, each time a little faster until she got the rhythm. Then she leaned back bracing herself on his thighs, taking him deeper still.

"God, why haven't we done this before?" she asked Nathan.

"No idea." He lifted when she came down pushing himself until he was balls deep in her. "Touch yourself. Make yourself come before I do."

She reached down and touched herself, rubbing like she'd felt Nathan do so many times before. Her body tightened, all her nerve endings alive. "Oh, God. Oh, God. Nathan!"

Her body convulsed around him, squeezing, pulsing, wringing his orgasm from him. She felt his seed shoot deep inside her.

She collapsed forward onto his chest. "Oh my!" She felt his heart bang against his chest.

"You were magnificent." He kissed her tenderly. "We should move."

"Did that already. Moved a lot."

He chuckled. "Yes, you did."

"We should do that again."

"Oh, we will. We most definitely will."

She rolled off him and cuddled into his side.

"I love you."

"I love you more," he said to her already sleeping form.

*****

Ella took over the morning chores that Nathan did. Milking the cows and gathering the eggs. He'd been very patient with her, teaching her how to milk the cow. It'd taken her a few tries to get the squeezing and pulling of the teets just right so the milk shot into the bucket and not on her feet.

The barn cats always gathered at milking time. Nathan was able to shoot milk at them and they loved it. Ella wasn't that talented so she brought down a bowl and filled it for them.

Learning how to gather the eggs had been easier. Just reach under the chicken and get the egg. Each chicken only laid one egg per day, so it was easy to just move down the row, moving chicken after chicken. Nathan set the chicken coop up so you could walk behind the chickens to gather the eggs. It made it less likely to get pecked if you took the eggs from behind.

It'd been six weeks, she was six and a half months pregnant and it was getting harder to get around. It was almost time for Nathan's cast to come off and he was doing a lot of his old chores, but Ella kept doing the ones she'd taken over. She enjoyed them and the time alone. It seemed like she never had time alone. She was always with someone, Martha, Nathan or one or more of the cowboys. But here, in the early morning, she could watch the sun rise as she went from the chicken coop to the barn. It was always magnificent. Today the moon hung low on the horizon. Clouds of bright orange and pink ran through a clear dark, blue sky. It humbled her to be in the presence of such wonder.

She sat on the milking stool, grabbed a teet and started to milk. Bessie didn't seem to even notice she was there, but kept chewing her cud and ignoring Ella. The cats were all there waiting for their milk. Even the new kittens had finally come down with their mama for the sweet treat. Ella put the bowl in the bucket and filled it first. She'd gotten pretty good at hitting just the bowl, but not always and she didn't want to waste any of the precious milk.

The cats scattering was the only warning Ella got that someone else was in the barn with her. She turned around and saw Daniel. Her heart pounded wildly in her chest, but she was determined not to let him know it.

"I wondered when you'd be back." She was proud of herself. Her voice didn't break revealing her fear. She kept milking the cow so he wouldn't see her hands shake.

"I've been watching, sweet sister. Watching and waiting until I could get you alone. Nathan kept coming with you every morning until this past week and finally, you started doing this alone."

"Why didn't you just go back to New York? What is it you want, Daniel?"

"I want everything. Everything, Father denied me. I'm the oldest. I should have inherited it all. But no. I wasn't legitimate. He'd already married your mother by the time I was born. It was

225

never an option for him to marry my mother. She wasn't rich enough. She wasn't rich at all. So he used her. Used her all those years."

"Sounds to me like he loved her. He kept going back to her when he didn't have to. It wasn't just for sex, he got that from my mother. No, he loved your mother and he loved you. You just didn't see it because of your greed and your jealousy." She finally stopped milking and turned toward him on the stool.

"You've gotten a lot bigger in the weeks since I saw you."

"Having a baby will do that to a person."

"Yes, well too bad. I don't relish killing a pregnant woman, but it's necessary. If you had just died in the buggy accident like you were supposed to, none of this would be needed."

"It's *not* necessary now. We can work something out Daniel. You don't have to kill me."

"Oh yes, I do. I have to kill you now and then go back and finish off Joshua. I should be able to get close to him, too. Just like I did you."

She shook her head. "No. No, you won't. I've warned him about you. Sent him a telegram after the accidents. But they weren't accidents were they? You sawed through the axle enough that a few rough patches on the road would break it. And you cut through the strap on Nathan's saddle, too, didn't you?"

Daniel laughed. Only then did she notice the gun he held.

"Yes. While you were sleeping. After having been such a gracious hostess, too. I met with the men I hired. They did the actual dirty work. I just watched and made sure it was done right."

"You could have shared with us. All you had to do was come forward. You have to have enough evidence to convince us, I believed you, and we would have shared with you. Why didn't you do that? Why this? Why kill us?"

"Because I want it all. It's all mine. For all the years that I was ignored. For all the time he spent with you and not me. I deserve it. All of it."

She rose slowly off the stool. Her growing bulk made it hard for her to get up, but now she didn't want to make any sudden moves for fear he'd kill her. "What now? You can't shoot me. The entire ranch would come running. You know no matter what you do, Nathan will find you. He'll kill you without so much as a backward thought."

"He'll never find me. I know I can't get the company now. You've taken everything from me. But I can still kill you. Then I'll go back to New York and kill Joshua. Neither of you will get anything either. You'll die knowing I won."

"You haven't won anything. You've only lost. Your greed is costing you everything. If you'd talked to Father, he would have included you. I know it."

He laughed again. This time the sound even more maniacal. It scared her. She didn't know how she'd keep him talking. Nathan would get worried if she didn't come back soon. He'd come looking for her. She just had to keep Daniel talking.

"Father didn't think anything of me."

"Not true. He sent you to school. Gave you the tools you needed to make a good life for yourself. Why didn't you do that?"

"Because I deserved more." He yelled at her. "I deserved everything."

Calmly, she picked up the bucket.

"What do you think you're doing? Put that down."

"I'm going to the house now, Daniel. I'm going to cook breakfast for my men."

"Do you think this is a game?" He raised the gun and pointed it at her. "Do you think I won't pull the trigger?"

"No. You won't pull it. You don't want to die. I know you don't."

"What do I have to live for? Tell me."

She walked toward him. "I don't know. Prison maybe." She threw the milk at him and then swung the bucket, connecting with his head. It wasn't heavy enough to do much damage, but it gave her time to run.

"Nathan!" she screamed running out of the

barn. "Nathan!"

Daniel fired a shot. She heard the blast and felt it as it whizzed past her. He fired again and again missed her.

She saw Nathan running toward her.

Daniel fired again. She felt the burning in her arm and stumbled to the ground.

She saw Nathan fire his Colt.

There was silence behind her.

Nathan was at her side. "Ella. Ella. Honey, talk to me."

She sat up and looked into her beloved's face. "He's behind me. He's trying to kill me. He's—"

"Dead."

"Dead? You killed him?"

"Yes. He won't be hurting us or anyone else ever again."

She burst into tears. "Thank God."

Nathan picked her up in his arms and carried her to the house. He went to the kitchen and put her down in one of the chairs at the table.

Martha wrapped her arms around Ella's shoulders.

"Ow."

"She's been shot in the shoulder," he said to Martha. "Let's get this dress off and see what we have."

Nathan tried to unbutton her dress, but his left hand didn't work well enough to open the tiny buttons.

"Here let me," said Martha, who made quick work of it.

"Looks like the shot just grazed your arm. You're going to be just fine."

"Thank God."

The baby kicked and she placed her hand on her stomach. "Oh, Nathan, feel. The baby wants us to know he's all right, too." She placed his hand on her belly. The baby kicked again and his father felt him for the first time.

The look of wonder on Nathan's face made Ella smile.

"It amazes me," he said. "Feeling him

kick."

"I know," said Ella. "But I'd prefer it if he didn't sit on my bladder." She punched on her stomach attempting to move the babe.

"Let's get you cleaned up," said Martha before turning around and getting the supplies.

After Ella's arm was cleaned and bandaged, she went to the bedroom and put on a clean dress.

Nathan followed her.

"Are you sure you're all right? It's a traumatic experience to be shot."

"I'm fine. I need to get back to work. I need for things to be normal."

"I sent one of the men to town for the sheriff. He'll take Daniel's body back to town and take statements from us. There shouldn't be any problem."

She nodded. "It's such a tragedy. He could have been part of the family, could have shared everything with us if he'd only tried. If he hadn't been so greedy. If he hadn't tried to kill us. If…."

"Ella, don't go thinking like that. Daniel

made his choices. None of them good ones. He wasn't right in the head and there's nothing you could have done differently that would have changed him."

"It's just so sad."

"I know, but you're safe and that's all that matters." He took her in his arms careful of her injury. "You're all that matters."

"Oh, Nathan, I love you so." She angled her head up for a kiss.

He obliged. Fierce. Gentle. His kiss was everything. She felt all his love in that kiss.

She gave all of hers back. He was her husband. Her mighty warrior. Her love.

EPILOGUE

Singing Bird arrived with no notice. She was just there one morning when Ella came to the kitchen. She and Nathan sat at the table. They both had cups in front of them.

"Singing Bird," said Ella, enveloping her mother-in-law in a hug. "I'm so glad you're here."

"I thought it should be close to your time and I wanted to be here for the birth of my grandchild."

"Son, Mother. A grandson," said Nathan

"You do not know this Nathan," admonished Singing Bird. "You could be having a little princess."

"As much as he fights with me, it must be a warrior," he laughed.

"Oh!" said Ella.

"What?" asked Nathan.

"I think we may be finding out sooner rather than later." She looked down at her feet. "My water just broke."

Nathan was on his feet and swooped her up in his arms before she could say another word.

"Mother, get the supplies we need. We're going to have a baby," he said as he carried Ella to their bedroom. He set her gently on her feet.

She unbuttoned her dress and dropped it to the floor. Her bloomers followed. She left on her chemise, needing some modesty.

Singing Bird came in a few minutes later carrying a pitcher of hot water. Martha followed with towels and scissors.

"We're ready. It's just a matter of waiting now for the little one to make its appearance," said Singing Bird.

"Ella's going to be just like an Arapaho woman. She won't make a sound as she gives birth," announced Nathan.

"Where did you get the idea that Arapaho women don't make noise when they give birth?"

"Well, that's what I was told and whenever the women of the village had babies, we never heard them."

"The men left the village or the women did. That's why you never heard anything. You are an idiot, my son, if you think we don't scream when we give birth. It is no different for us than for a white woman. If Ella wants to scream, she will scream."

"Stop arguing both of you and send for the doctor. I want the doctor here."

"I already sent one of the men to fetch him," said Martha.

"He should be here in an hour or so, if he's in the office."

"If he is not," said Singing Bird as she brushed Ella's hair back from her face. "I have assisted in many births. You will not be alone in this, my daughter."

Ella was calmed by Singing Bird's words and settled back to wait for the birth of her child. The first pain hit hard. It took her breath away. She'd barely had time to catch it when the next pain came. And so it went, every five minutes for the first few hours.

The doctor wasn't in the office and so their man left a message for him with his wife. He was out on another birth, but would come as soon as he could.

Nathan felt helpless. He hated seeing Ella go through so much pain. When the contractions started coming every two minutes or so, he almost had to be escorted from the room.

"If you can't maintain control of yourself, you must leave," said his mother. "Ella needs you to be strong."

Nathan nodded and buried his worry. Singing Bird would take care of Ella. He placed his faith in his mother.

He sat by Ella's side holding her hand.

"You should leave now Nathan. You can do nothing more here and should not see it when she gives birth."

"I'm staying. Ella needs me."

Ella looked up at Nathan and squeezed his hand. "I'm scared."

"You'll be fine. You're young and strong. You got shot for heaven's sake and came through that just fine. You will this too."

"It is time. Ella you need to push now. Push very hard," said Singing Bird.

Ella beared down, pushing as hard as she could. Then she had to stop and catch her breath. Her body was ready for this baby to come and she pushed again. Again and again she pushed until the little one slid out into his grandmother's waiting hands.

"You have a son. A fine young warrior." Singing Bird quickly tied off and cut the umbilical cord then handed the baby to Martha who took it and cleaned it up.

When she was done, she handed the baby to Ella.

Ella took her newborn son and opened the blanket to see him. He was beautiful. A carbon copy of his father with blue eyes and midnight black hair. He had all his toes and fingers. She counted just to make sure.

"You have said nothing, my son. Congratulate your wife on a job well done."

Nathan looked from Ella to the baby and back again. Then he reached down and took one of the tiny hands with his fingers. The baby grabbed his father's finger. Nathan looked at Ella and grinned. "Thank you. Thank you for loving me. Thank you for my son." He kissed her so softly, she thought she would cry from the tenderness of it.

"I love you. You've given me everything I could ever want. A home. A baby and most especially, you my love," she said through her tears of joy.

He rested his head on top of hers. Together they watched their baby until he started to fuss.

Ella put him to her breast and helped him find her nipple. He latched on and began to suckle.

"What shall we name him?" asked Nathan.

"I was thinking that maybe we could name him after our fathers."

"Robert Benjamin Ravenclaw it is."

The three of them fell asleep. Nathan holding Ella and she the baby. A family for all time.

ABOUT THE AUTHOR

Cynthia Woolf was born in Denver, Colorado and raised in the mountains west of Golden. She spent her early years running wild around the mountain side with her friends.

Their closest neighbor was one quarter of a mile away, so her little brother was her playmate and her best friend. That fierce friendship lasted until his death in 2006. Cynthia was and is an avid reader. Her mother was a librarian and brought new books home each week. This is where young Cynthia first got the storytelling bug. She wrote her first story at the age of ten. A romance about a little boy she liked at the time.

She worked her way through college and went to work full time straight after graduation and there was little time to write. Then in 1990 she and two friends started a round robin writing a story about pirates. She found that she missed the writing and kept on with other stories. In 1992 she joined Colorado Romance Writers and

Romance Writers of America. Unfortunately, the loss of her job demanded she not renew her memberships and her writing stagnated for many years.

In 2001, she saw an ad in the paper for a writers conference being put on by CRW and decided she'd attend. One of her favorite authors, Catherine Coulter, was the keynote speaker. Cynthia was lucky enough to have a seat at Ms. Coulter's table at the luncheon and after talking with her, decided she needed to get back to her writing. She rejoined both CRW and RWA that day and hasn't looked back.

Cynthia credits her wonderfully supportive husband Jim and the great friends she's made at CRW for saving her sanity and allowing her to explore her creativity.

OTHER TITLES AVAILABLE

CENTAURI DAWN

CENTAURI TWILIGHT

CENTAURI MIDNIGHT

TAME A WILD HEART

TAME A WILD WIND

TAME A WILD BRIDE

THE SWORDS OF GREGARA – JENALA

THE SWORDS OF GREGARA – RIZA

THE SWORDS OF GREGARA - HONORA

CAPITAL BRIDE

HEIRESS BRIDE

COMING SOON

FIERY BRIDE

Printed in Great Britain
by Amazon.co.uk, Ltd.,
Marston Gate.